This couldn't be happening . . .

The reception desk at the Green Falls Inn was polished wood, with an old-fashioned telephone on it. Cat could see herself standing behind it, greeting guests, answering the phone.

"What are you doing?" a harsh voice asked.

Cat turned her head. A woman with a face like a prune stood there.

Cat smiled brightly. "Is Sally Layton around? I'm supposed to see her about a job here."

"I'm Miss Andrews, the housekeeper." She surveyed Cat and shook her head. "You don't look like you're going to be much of a maid."

Cat couldn't have heard correctly. "Did you say – a maid?"

"Your hours are three-thirty to five-thirty, Monday, Wednesday and Friday. You will report to me. Be on time."

Cat swallowed. "What – what exactly will I be doing?"

"What do you think a maid does? You'll sweep, dust, mop. . ."

The horrid words continued to come, but Cat wasn't hearing them any more. She was in a state of shock.

Titles by Marilyn Kaye available in Lions

THREE OF A KIND

1. With Friends Like These, Who Needs Enemies?
2. Home's a Nice Place to Visit,
   But I Wouldn't Want to Live There
3. Will the Real Becka Morgan Please Stand Up?
4. Two's Company, Four's a Crowd
5. Cat Morgan, Working Girl

SISTERS

Phoebe
Cassie
Daphne
Lydia

A Friend Like Phoebe

Cat Morgan, Working Girl

Marilyn Kaye

Lions

Lions, an imprint of HarperCollins *Children's Books*

For Amy Cimino

First published in the U.S. in 1991
by HarperCollins Books.
First published in the U.K. in Lions in 1992

Lions is an imprint of
HarperCollins Children's Books,
part of HarperCollins Publishers Ltd,
77-85 Fulham Palace Road,
Hammersmith, London W6 8JB

Printed and bound in Great Britain by
HarperCollins Manufacturing Ltd, Glasgow

One

Josie Morgan lay sprawled on the living room floor with the *Green Falls Daily News* spread out in front of her. She pushed her unruly red hair out of her eyes and examined the front page. Scanning the headlines, she grimaced. There was a war going on in a country she'd never heard of, crime rates were up right here in Vermont, and a five car pile-up on a road just outside Green Falls had resulted in a lot of injuries.

"Why isn't there any good news?" she muttered.

"Ick!" Cat Morgan exclaimed from her place on the couch. She was also reading the paper. "This is disgusting!"

"No kidding," Josie agreed. "Wars, bank robberies, car accidents . . ."

"That's not what I mean," Cat said. "Look at my hands!"

Josie looked. Cat's fingers had black smudges on them. Josie had the same smudges on her own hands.

"I knew there was a good reason not to read

5

the newspaper," Cat grumbled, gazing at her dirty hands in dismay.

Swaying in the rocking chair, Becka Morgan glanced up from *her* newspaper. "It's not permanent, Cat. It comes off with soap and water."

"Maybe I don't particularly feel like washing my hands every time I turn a page," Cat replied. As she spoke, she automatically smoothed back a lock of hair that had escaped from her barrette. Then she let out a little shriek. "Oh, no! Now it's in my hair, too!"

"That's okay," Josie said cheerfully. "Your hair's as black as the ink. It won't even show."

"But I'll know it's there," Cat moaned. "And I just washed it this morning." With her hands stretched stiffly out in front of her, she rose from the couch and hurried to the little bathroom off the hallway.

"This is interesting," Becka said, turning back to the newspaper. "The public library is having a special exhibit of books by authors from Vermont."

Josie made no response. Only Becka would find something like that interesting. Bored and depressed with all the grim headlines, Josie pushed page after page aside. Then she brightened. "Hey, here's something good!"

"What?" Becka asked.

"The Giants have traded Rob Fenster to the Patriots!"

"Huh?"

"Football," Josie explained.

"Oh."

Josie turned another page. Then she started laughing.

"What's so funny?" Cat asked, returning with clean hands.

"This ad on page twenty-six," Josie replied. "Listen to this: 'An amazing scientific breakthrough! Now you can get rid of unsightly freckles and birthmarks. Use this remarkable *Invisicream* daily and watch those spots disappear!'"

Cat picked up her copy with two fingers and gingerly turned the page. "Why don't you get some of that stuff?"

"What for?" Josie asked.

"To get rid of your freckles, dummy."

"Maybe I like my freckles," Josie retorted.

Becka slipped off the rocking chair and went to the mirror that hung over the fireplace. She touched a tiny brown mark on her chin. "I wonder if that *Invisicream* would make this birthmark disappear."

Josie rolled her eyes. "Becka, *Invisicream* doesn't work. Nothing gets rid of freckles and birthmarks."

"Then why would it say that?"

"Because they're trying to get you to buy the stuff. It's all made up."

"How can you be sure?" Becka was still studying her birthmark. "It's in a newspaper. A newspaper wouldn't print something that's not true."

Josie eyed her impatiently. Becka could be so naïve sometimes. "It's an *ad*, Becka. Somebody paid to have this put in the newspaper."

Becka went back to the rocking chair. "I still don't think it would be in there if it wasn't true. Newspapers don't lie. I should know. I work for a newspaper."

Cat directed scornful eyes at her. "The *Green Gazette*'s not a real newspaper."

"Sure it is," Becka said. "Just because it's only for Green Falls Junior High doesn't mean it's not a real newspaper. We even take ads."

"Personally, I like the ads best," Cat remarked. "Like this one, on page six."

Josie turned to page six.

"Are you talking about this ad for Danielle's Boutique?" It was a photo of three girls wearing fancy dresses.

"Check out the dress in the middle," Cat said. "Isn't it gorgeous?"

Josie shrugged. A dress was a dress to her – something she was occasionally forced to wear instead of jeans.

A wistful sigh escaped Cat's lips. "I think it's positively elegant. It would be so perfect for the Turnaround."

"The *what?*" Josie asked.

"The Turnaround. It's a dance the pep club's going to have next month. Girls are supposed to ask boys for dates."

"Oh." Josie lost interest. Dances appealed to her about as much as dresses. Just last month, she and her friend Red MacPherson had almost gotten conned into going to one. Luckily, they had escaped in the nick of time.

"I love this dress," Cat said dreamily. "Black velvet, white lace collar, dropped waist . . ."

Josie tuned Cat out. Becka didn't seem to be listening either. She was engrossed in a newspaper article.

Well, that isn't surprising, Josie thought. Becka would read anything. An earthquake could hit and she wouldn't notice. When she wasn't reading, she was daydreaming about what she'd read. Josie could never understand that. She'd much rather do things than read about them.

If Becka was puzzling to her, Cat was mystifying. All she cared about was how she looked, what she wore, who she dated. Who would ever guess the three of them were related? Looking at them wouldn't give anyone a clue.

Becka had fair, frizzy hair and a penchant for crazy, gypsyish clothes. Cat had glossy black hair and emerald green eyes. She was always perfectly groomed and dressed in the latest fashion. As for herself . . . *how would*

9

I describe myself? Josie wondered. Tall, lanky, short red hair, and perpetually skinned knees from playing basketball. Luckily, they were almost always hidden by the faded blue jeans she wore.

About the only thing they had in common was their age – thirteen – and their last name. Of course, there was no reason why they should look alike, act alike, *be* alike, even though they were all Morgans. Only five months ago, they had been unrelated orphans. Then Annie and Ben Morgan had come along and adopted all three of them. Practically overnight, they went from being orphanage roommates to sisters.

Josie heard the back door of the house slam. A moment later, Annie Morgan appeared in the room. The fresh, multi-coloured smudges on her smock announced that she'd been out in her studio, painting. "Hi, girls," she called. Her eyebrows went up as she saw what they were doing. "Since when have you guys become newspaper readers?"

Cat answered for them. "Since the principal started requiring it. We're supposed to read the paper every day. Can you believe it? How could he do this to us?"

"Well, it's not exactly torture to read a newspaper," Annie replied.

"It is for me," Cat murmured.

Becka explained, "Dr Potter decided we should all be more aware of current events. He thinks we waste time in homeroom, so from now on we'll spend the period talking about the news."

"It's so ridiculous," Cat said. "*I* don't waste time in homeroom."

"What do you do there?" Josie asked. "Add another layer of eye shadow?"

Cat made a face at her, but she didn't argue. *Probably because it's true*, Josie thought.

Annie perched on the arm of the couch, and Cat looked up at her hopefully. "Maybe you could write our teachers a note to get us out of it. Like, you could say the news is too violent or something."

Annie laughed. "No way, honey. I think Dr Potter's idea is excellent. We should all be aware of what's going on in the world."

"But everything that's going on is so depressing," Josie complained.

"That's not true," Becka said. "There's an article on page ten about how the standard of living has improved in eastern Europe. It's fascinating."

"Maybe if you live in eastern Europe," Cat countered. "We live in Green Falls, Vermont."

"Now, Cat," Annie gently reprimanded her. "We're all people, and we need to care about what happens to people all over the world.

Come on, I'll bet there's something in this newspaper you'd enjoy reading about."

Cat considered that. "Actually, I did find something interesting." She held up the ad for Danielle's Boutique. "Isn't this dress pretty?"

"Very pretty," Annie agreed.

"It would be nice for a special, dress-up occasion, wouldn't it?" Cat said casually. Then she snapped her fingers. "I almost forgot! The pep club's having a dance next month!"

Josie and Becka exchanged looks. Cat was never good at being subtle. Annie looked at her in amusement. But she shook her head. "It's also pretty expensive, Cat."

Cat dropped her innocent act. "Seventy-five dollars isn't so much for a really nice dress," she objected. "And it's going to be a very special dance, Annie. Everyone's going to get really dressed up."

Annie's face became serious. "Cat, I'd love to be able to get you that dress. But—"

Before she could get any further, the front door opened and Ben Morgan came in. For a moment, he just stood there, very still.

"Ben, what's the matter?" Annie asked in alarm.

A slow smile spread across his face. "Nothing. I'm just taking a minute to absorb this happy scene. Home sweet home, and all my

12

lovely ladies together. It's a very nice change after a day in Morgan's Country Foods."

Josie grinned. "Didn't any lovely ladies come into the store this afternoon?"

"No ladies at all, lovely or otherwise," Ben told her. "No men either, for that matter."

"Ben!" Annie exclaimed. "Are you saying we had no customers at all?"

Ben pulled off his jacket. "Okay, I'm exaggerating. Maybe we had two or three." He was still smiling, but Josie detected little lines of concern around his eyes.

Annie got up and went to the window. "Maybe it's the weather. It's been awfully cold today, and it looks like snow. Some people don't like to go out much in the winter."

"They still have to eat," Ben said. "What I don't understand is the maple syrup. Sales have been really low. Don't people eat pancakes and French toast any more?"

"Of course they do," Annie replied. "But I guess they're buying their maple syrup somewhere else."

"All sales are down," Ben said. He joined her at the window. "We need to do bills today."

"Do we have to?" Annie sighed.

"Mmm-hmm. The mortgage is due. And the home-improvement loan payment. I think we should go over the budget, too. The heating bills have been staggering."

Hearing this conversation made Josie uneasy. She got the feeling her parents wanted to talk privately. "I'm going upstairs," she announced, gathering up her newspaper.

Becka had picked up on the atmosphere, too. "I'll come with you."

Only Cat seemed totally unaware of what was going on. She stayed where she was, still looking at the dress ad. "Cat," Josie said, "we're going upstairs."

"Mmm."

Becka leaned over the couch. "Come with us and I'll tell you what's in the newspaper. Then you won't have to read it." That got a response. Cat left the couch and followed them upstairs.

They all had their own rooms now. When they'd first been adopted, there had been only one bedroom available for them in the old, slightly ramshackle farmhouse. Becka had gotten the next renovated room. Just two weeks ago, Ben had finished painting the third. Cat had made a big show of graciously offering the new bedroom to Josie. It hadn't been all that generous, considering that the original bedroom was twice the size of the new one.

The three girls gathered in Cat's room. Becka climbed onto the bed and curled up, wrapping her arms around her knees. Her eyes were dark with worry. "Do you think Annie and Ben are having money problems?"

"It sure sounds like it," Josie said. "Maybe it's just a temporary thing."

"What are you talking about?" Cat asked.

"Annie and Ben," Becka said. "Didn't you hear what they were saying just now?"

"They were talking about maple syrup."

Josie groaned. "Where do you think our money comes from? Believe it or not, Cat, it doesn't grow on trees."

Cat sighed. "I guess there's no point in bugging them about this dress, then."

Josie felt like she was about to explode. "Honestly, Cat, you're so greedy!"

That accusation didn't bother Cat. She'd heard it before. She twisted the little ruby ring on her finger. "I wonder how much this is worth."

"Cat!" Becka gasped. "You wouldn't sell your ring for a dress, would you?"

Josie was a little shocked, too. Even though she wasn't into jewellery, the identical ruby rings they all wore were special. Annie and Ben had given the rings to them as a symbol of their birth as a family.

"No, I guess not," Cat admitted.

Josie tossed the newspaper on the bed.

"Hey, don't get that nasty black ink on my bedspread," Cat warned.

Josie wasn't listening. Something on the back page of the paper had caught her eye and she snatched it back up. She read the ad in the For Sale column and she whistled.

"What is it?" Becka asked.

"Listen to this: 'For sale. One gelding quarter horse, ten years old, sixteen hands.' "

"Sixteen hands!" Cat exclaimed. "He must be deformed!"

Josie shot her a scathing look. "No, dummy, that's how horses are measured. Wow, would I love a horse like that."

"We've already got a horse," Becka pointed out.

"Maybelline?" Josie shook her head. "She's a sweet old nag, and I love her, but you guys don't ride her and I do. She can barely move."

"How much does that horse cost?" Becka asked.

Josie smiled. "Only four hundred dollars. That's really cheap."

"Four hundred dollars!" Cat yelled. "And you're calling *me* greedy?"

Becka was taken aback, too. "You can't ask Annie and Ben for four hundred dollars, Josie. Not when they're worried about money."

"Don't be silly. I'm not planning to ask them for any money," Josie assured her sisters. Still, she couldn't help wondering what colour the horse was.

"Okay, Becka, tell me what's in the newspaper," Cat demanded.

As Becka launched into a lecture on eastern Europe, Josie looked at the ad again. For as long as she could remember, she'd wanted a horse of her own. A lively, spirited horse who could jump over fences, take her galloping across the fields . . . but where in the world would she ever find four hundred dollars?

Maybe there was a cheaper horse for sale. She scanned the listings. There weren't that many, and before long she realised she was looking at the wanted ads. One of them caught her eye.

WANTED: Companion for elderly woman, ten hours weekly, five dollars an hour. Student preferred. For more information, call Mrs Daley.

A tingle shot through her. Ten hours a week at five dollars an hour. That meant fifty dollars a week. She did some rapid calculations. In eight weeks she could have four hundred dollars.

Stop it, Josie scolded herself. Whoever this elderly woman was, she probably wanted someone older, more experienced, not a thirteen-year-old eighth-grader. Even if the woman did offer her the job, Annie and Ben might not give her permission to take it. Besides, she had school, homework, basketball practice, work at the store, chores at home – when would she have time for a part-time job?

Still, it wouldn't hurt to ask Annie and Ben. And she could call this Mrs Daley for more information.

"I'm going to help Annie with dinner," she announced. Carefully, she tore out the ads for the horse and the job and stuck them in her jeans.

Two

At Cat's lunch table, the main topic of conversation was the same as it had been the day before, and the day before that.

"I don't know who to ask to the Turnaround." Sharon Cohen said.

"Me neither," Karen Hall echoed.

"I think I'm going to ask Alex Hayes," Britt Foley announced.

"Why?" Marla Eastman asked.

"Three reasons," Britt replied. "He's not going with anyone, he's taller than I am, and I'm pretty sure he'll say yes."

Trisha Heller clutched her throat. "What if you asked a guy and he said no?"

"I'd die," Sharon and Karen said simultaneously.

Cat shuddered along with the rest of them, although personally, she couldn't imagine anything like that ever happening to her.

"I might ask Jeff Wilson," Marla mused. "Who are you going to ask, Cat?"

"I haven't decided yet." Cat surveyed the noisy, crowded cafeteria. There were plenty of guys around, but none of them grabbed her eye.

"Well, I've got some news that might help you decide," Britt said. "I heard something very interesting last period." Britt glanced at another table. The others turned, too, and Cat knew immediately who Britt meant. Heather Beaumont sat there, surrounded by her usual group of adoring fans.

"Don't keep us in suspense," Marla ordered. "Tell!"

Britt leaned across the table, and the other girls automatically moved in closer. "I was talking to Pam Wooster. You know, she's on the tennis team with Eve Dedham. Wait till you hear what Eve told her."

She paused again and smiled mysteriously. Cat could tell that Britt was enjoying this and wanted to drag it out as long as possible. "Come on," she said impatiently. "Get to the point."

"Okay. Eve told Pam that Heather and Todd had a serious fight at Luigi's yesterday. And Pam said that Eve thinks she's going to break up with him."

Cat studied her fingernails. "What does that have to do with who I take to the Turnaround?"

The others gave her reproving looks. "Get real, Cat," Marla said. "He was your boyfriend."

It was a totally unnecessary reminder. *"Was,"*

Cat said. "Past tense. I wouldn't take Todd Murphy back on a silver platter."

She meant it, too. In the ongoing war between Cat and Heather Beaumont, Todd had been a major weapon. But even before Heather had managed to lure him away in the last battle, Cat had been getting bored with him.

She took another look at the pretty blonde holding court just three tables away. She had to admit, Todd's main appeal had been the fact that he was Heather's boyfriend when Cat first came to Green Falls. But if Heather had no use for him any more, why should she?

The others still looked sceptical. "I've got more important things on my mind right now," Cat told them. "Like, what I'm going to wear to the Turnaround. I saw a fabulous dress in the newspaper yesterday, but it's really expensive." She sighed. "I wish I was old enough to get a part-time job."

"I know what you mean," Marla agreed. "My sister just got an after-school job. She's going to be making tons of money, not to mention the discount."

"What discount?" Britt asked.

"She's working at Danielle's Boutique, and she gets a twenty per cent discount on anything she buys there."

"Danielle's Boutique!" Cat exclaimed. "Marla, that's where my dress is! Quick, somebody, what's twenty per cent off seventy-five dollars?"

Trisha, the maths wizard, whipped out a pencil and did a quick calculation on her napkin. "Sixty dollars," she announced.

Cat groaned. "It's still way too much."

"It wouldn't matter anyway," Marla said. "Chris isn't supposed to buy stuff with the discount for anyone but herself. She won't even get me anything."

"Danielle's gives credit," Karen said. "You get three weeks to pay it off and you only have to put ten per cent down. That's – what?"

"Seven dollars and fifty cents," Trisha stated.

"I can come up with *that*," Cat said, "but where am I going to get . . . how much, Trisha?"

"Sixty-seven dollars and fifty cents."

"Right. How can I come up with sixty-seven dollars and fifty cents in three weeks? How do kids our age make money?"

"There's baby-sitting," Marla suggested.

Cat wrinkled her nose. "Little kids. Ugh."

"Dog walking?" Karen offered.

That appealed to Cat about as much as baby-sitting.

"My brother shovels snow," Sharon mentioned.

Britt giggled. "Cat couldn't do that. She'd ruin her nails."

"Very funny," Cat retorted. She leaned back in her chair. "I wonder who Heather's going to take to the Turnaround if she breaks up with Todd?"

Marla grinned. "She's probably waiting to find out who you want to ask, and then she'll ask him first."

"That sounds like something she'd do," Cat murmured. "Hey, that's not such a bad idea. Maybe *I'll* find out who she's planning to ask."

"Shh," Trisha whispered. "Here she comes."

Heather, accompanied by two friends, passed their table, but she didn't even glance at them. So she didn't see the piece of paper that flew out of her notebook and landed on the floor right by Cat.

Cat scooped it up. It was a newspaper clipping. She frowned as she studied it. "Why would Heather be interested in oil prices?"

"Check out the other side," Trisha said.

Cat turned it over. Then she practically choked. "This is it! My dress!" She showed the ad for Danielle's Boutique to the others. "It's the one in the middle."

"It's gorgeous," Marla exclaimed. She peered closer. "There's a little check mark over it."

"I'll bet Heather's planning to buy it," Britt said.

Cat wanted to cry. "She can't! It's mine!"

"Not unless you buy it before she does," Marla said. "You and Heather are probably around the same size. And Chris told me

Danielle's only orders one or two dresses in each size."

"Oh, well," Britt said, "you wouldn't want to show up in the same dress she's wearing anyway."

Cat gritted her teeth. "I want that dress. I'm going to Danielle's this afternoon and putting it aside."

"But how are you going to get the rest of the money in three weeks?" Marla asked.

"I don't know," Cat said. "I'll find a way." She would, too. If she wanted something badly enough, she could always figure out a way to get it. And knowing Heather was interested in this dress made her want it even more.

When the last bell rang, Becka hurried out of class. She had a *Green Gazette* meeting, and there was something she had to do first.

She ducked into a rest room, went directly to a mirror, and examined the birthmark on her chin. She couldn't see any change in it yet. Maybe it was too soon. She'd only just bought the *Invisicream*.

Funny, that birthmark had never bothered her before. But just a week ago, when she was working at the store, a small child had asked, "What's that spot on your chin?" Ever since then, it had looked bigger and darker to her.

She got the silver tube out of her purse and

24

squeezed a little cream out. She dabbed it on her chin and rubbed it in. She dropped the tube back in her purse just in time. The rest room door swung open and Josie burst in.

"Hi," she said hurriedly to Becka.

Becka's mouth fell open as Josie pulled off her jeans. She whipped a skirt out of her knapsack and put it on. Becka couldn't remember the last time she'd seen Josie in a skirt.

"What are you doing?"

"I've got an interview," Josie said. "There's an old lady who wants a part-time companion. Ben and Annie said I could apply. If I get hired, I'll get five dollars an hour. I could have enough for that horse in eight weeks!"

She washed her hands and ran back to the door. "Wish me luck," she yelled as she tore out.

Becka didn't. She stood there and shook her head in annoyance. Her sisters were so selfish. All Cat could think about was getting money for a dress. Josie wanted money for a horse. No one seemed to care that the Morgan *family* was having money problems. Except her. And she couldn't think of anything to do to help them.

By the time she got to the *Green Gazette* meeting, it had already started. Jason Wister, the editor of the newspaper, was handing out story assignments.

"Tom, can you catch a ride on the bus with

25

the football team Friday to cover the game?"

"Yeah. Can I take photos, too?"

"Sure," Jason said. "Take as many as you want. But they won't go in the newspaper. We don't have any money in the budget for photos."

A chorus of groans filled the room. "A newspaper without any pictures looks so crummy," someone said.

"I know," Jason replied. "But we can't afford them unless we have more money to spend. And the only way we can get more money is if we sell more ad space. If you guys would work harder at soliciting ads, we could have pictures."

"How are we supposed to solicit ads?" One of the students asked.

"Just go around to businesses and stores and ask them. Tell them how an ad can improve their business, increase their sales, that sort of thing."

"It really works," one girl piped up. "My mother bakes fancy cakes for special occasions, like weddings and birthdays. She took an ad in the *Gazette* last year, and kids must have shown it to their parents, because she got a lot more orders."

Becka sat up straight. That was what Annie and Ben needed – advertising! Why hadn't she thought of that before? If it worked for birthday

26

cakes, it would work for a food store.

Her mind was reeling. Some people in town probably didn't even know the store was there. One little advertisement would get people to start thinking about Morgan's Country Foods. They'd come out of curiosity, if nothing else, and end up buying. Sales would skyrocket!

She leaned back in her seat with a pleased smile. She, Becka Morgan, was going to help make the Morgan family fortune.

Standing on the doorstep of a pretty, well-kept cottage, Josie took a moment to smooth down her hair and pull up her knee socks. She took a deep breath and pressed the doorbell.

The woman who answered the door couldn't have been Mrs Daley. She was an attractive, fair-haired woman in jeans and a flannel shirt.

"Hi, I'm Josie Morgan. I called about the job."

"Oh yes, come on in, Josie." Josie entered the house and looked around curiously. It was an old-fashioned-looking room, with large, dark, carved furniture. There was a big oriental rug on the floor.

"I'm Sue Campbell, Mrs Daley's companion."

Josie's face fell. "Oh no, you mean, she's already hired someone?"

The woman smiled. "No, I'm the full-time

companion. We're looking for someone to come in for a couple of hours, a few days a week, to stay with Mrs Daley while I do the grocery shopping, run errands, that sort of thing."

"Oh, I see." Josie decided Mrs Daley must be pretty decrepit, if she needed someone with her every minute. "Is Mrs Daley . . . very old, Miss Campbell?"

"Call me Sue. As for Mrs Daley, old . . . ? Well, in some ways, yes. In other ways, not at all."

Josie found out what she meant soon enough.

"Is that the child who's come about the job?" A tiny woman stood under the arch leading to the next room.

Josie bristled at being called a child. But she supposed that, compared to this woman, she was a child.

Her hair was grey, and she walked with a cane. Moving very slowly, leaning heavily on the cane, she approached Josie. "Let me take a look at you."

While she did, Josie took the opportunity to look *her* over. Her grey hair was almost as wild and unruly as Josie's. She wore baggy trousers and an old sweater with holes that had been darned. She looked sort of shabby, and Josie wondered how she could afford a full-time companion.

"I'll bet you're an athlete," Mrs Daley stated.

Startled, Josie nodded. "Yes, I play basketball for Green Falls Junior High. How could you tell?"

"Scabby knees," Mrs Daley said. "I always had scabby knees when I was your age. What's your favourite basketball team?"

"Uh, the Celtics."

"Mine, too!"

Josie gaped at her. Mrs Daley's eyes were as bright and lively as a child's. "What are you wearing that skirt for?" the elderly woman demanded. "Your legs must be freezing."

"I . . . I thought you might want someone who dresses nicely."

"Nonsense," Mrs Daley barked. "A good, heavy pair of jeans is what I want to see you in. You have jeans, I presume?"

Josie nodded. "That's usually all I ever wear."

"Good." She peered at Josie's face closely. "Aha! You don't wear make-up."

"Well, no, I—"

"Excellent! I'm tired of seeing these young girls messing themselves up with all that junk. Now, would this job interfere with your schoolwork?"

"I don't think so."

"How about your sports?"

"I guess it depends on when you'd need me," Josie replied.

"We're pretty flexible around here. We aim to please. Isn't that right, Sue?"

"Yes, ma'am," Sue replied with a twinkle in her eye.

"Don't *ma'am* me," Mrs Daley snapped. "You're going to frighten this child. She'll think I'm some sort of tyrant, and she won't want to come work here. Do you want to work here? What's your name, anyway?"

"Josie. Josie Morgan, ma'am." The *ma'am* slipped out before she could stop it. Mrs Daley grimaced, but then she grinned.

"Well, I suppose that's all right. Respect's a good thing for a young person to have. Don't see much of it these days." She paused. "Josie. I like that. It's not one of these fancy, newfangled names. It's got a good, solid sound. Well, Josie Morgan, you want this job?"

Josie's head was spinning. "I . . . I guess that depends. What would you want me to do?"

"You'd be a companion. That means you keep me company. You a good reader?"

"Okay, I guess."

"Good. My eyes don't work the way they used to. Can you fix a cup of tea?"

Dumbly, Josie nodded.

"Wash windows?"

Josie looked at her in dismay. Mrs Daley's lips twitched, then she burst out laughing.

"That was a joke, my dear." She turned to

Sue. "I think she'll do. What do you think?"

Sue smiled warmly. "I think she'll do just fine."

Josie could tell from the way Sue looked at Mrs Daley that there was real affection between them. She wasn't surprised. Once she recovered from her surprise at the oddness of this old lady, she had an idea she'd feel the same.

They worked out a schedule of two hours after school three days a week, and four hours on Saturday. Josie left with the promise that she'd be back the following day.

She wanted to race home and tell everyone, but there was something else she wanted to do first. She stopped at the nearest pay phone and reached in her pocket for the ad.

She stuck in her coin and dialled the number. "Hello, my name is Josie Morgan. I'm calling about the horse you have for sale. Could I come over and see him?"

She got directions from the person on the other end of the line and hung up. Her heart was thumping as she started walking. What if he wasn't the horse of her dreams? What if he was lazy and slow, or wild and unmanageable?

No, it wasn't possible. Somehow, she just knew it. Everything else was working out perfectly. This horse was going to be perfect, too.

Three

"She's nothing like what I expected," Josie told Annie several days later as they cut up vegetables for a salad. "She's so . . . different."

"How?" Annie asked.

"Well, I thought old people were all cranky and mean and out of it. Mrs Daley's totally real. She's into basketball, and she likes action movies, and she's funny. She's more like a friend than a boss."

"She sounds like an interesting person," Annie said. "I'd like to meet her sometime. Does she have any family here in Green Falls?"

"I don't think so," Josie replied. "At least, no one ever comes to visit while I'm there. And if she had family, she wouldn't need a paid companion." She tossed a mound of cucumbers into the salad bowl. "Working for her doesn't seem like work. I have such a good time, I feel funny taking money from her."

Annie paused in the middle of cutting up a tomato. "Are you sure it's not interfering with your schoolwork?"

Josie began measuring out oil for the salad

dressing. "No. In fact, I think it helps. I made a schedule, and I'm sticking to it."

"What about basketball practice?"

Josie grinned. "That's no problem. Some parents have been complaining to Coach Meadows about all the time we spend in practice. So he cut it back to just Tuesday and Thursday afternoons. I'm working at Mrs Daley's Monday, Wednesday, Friday, and Saturday afternoon. So it's perfect!" She took a piece of lettuce and dipped it into her dressing. "Try this. Does it need anything?"

Annie popped the lettuce into her mouth. "It's delicious. I don't know how you do it. Whenever I make dressing, it's either too oily or too vinegary. Has Mrs Daley discovered your culinary expertise?"

"My what?"

"Your talent in the kitchen."

"Not yet," Josie told her. "She doesn't eat much. She says her taste buds don't work the way they used to. I want to come up with something that appeals to her." She considered it. "Maybe a cheese soufflé."

Annie gazed at her lovingly. "You're some girl, Josie Morgan. I'm proud of you."

Josie blushed. "Thanks."

"Now, what are you going to do with all that money you're making?"

This was the perfect time to tell her about the

horse. She was just about to when Ben walked in. "Something smells unbelievably fantastic in here. Could it be . . . is it possible that we're having what I think we're having?"

"It's Josie's lasagna with her special secret sauce," Annie informed him. Ben clutched the sink and pretended he was about to faint with delight.

Annie gave Ben a look of mock frustration. "Would you believe that she won't even tell *me* what's in it?"

"Mrs Parker made me promise," Josie apologised. She remembered the day that the Willoughby Hall cook taught her the recipe, then swore her to secrecy.

Ben ruffled Josie's hair. "Well, as long as you're here to cook it, we don't need to know. But maybe when you go away to college—"

"I'll ask Mrs Parker," Josie promised.

Ben took a deep whiff of the aroma coming from the stove. "Sally and George are in for a treat. By the way, what time are they coming?"

"Around seven," Annie said.

"Good. I'll have time for a shower, a change, and maybe even a little nap."

"Rough day?" Josie asked.

"Boring day," Ben replied. "You know, sometimes sitting and doing nothing in an empty store is more exhausting than waiting on a hundred customers."

34

The sparkle in Annie's eyes seemed to dim. "Business hasn't picked up?"

Becka came into the kitchen just in time to catch that. "Don't worry," she said. "When our ad comes out in the *Green Gazette*, we'll have more business than we can handle. Have you written it yet, Ben?"

Ben closed his eyes and hit himself on the side of the head. "I forgot. I'm sorry, Becka."

Becka put her hands on her hips and eyed him sternly. "I want you to do it right away. Ben, you used to be in advertising back in New York. You must know how powerful a well-developed advertisement can be."

Ben looked at her in amusement. "How do you know so much about advertising all of a sudden?"

"I found some of your old advertising magazines up in the attic and I've been reading them. It's fascinating! Why do people buy one brand of toothpaste instead of another that's exactly the same? Because of the advertising! It makes the customer *think* one brand is better."

"I know, I know," Ben said. "I remember it well. Boy, am I glad to be out of that business. But I'll write your ad right away," he added hastily. "As soon as I've had a shower."

"I'll go set the table," Becka said and went back out into the dining room.

"Business will get better," Annie assured Ben.

"I hope so. For all our sakes." He took one last long sniff and left.

"Josie? What's wrong?"

"Huh? Oh, nothing." She felt Annie's eyes on her. She busied herself chopping a garlic clove and turned away so Annie couldn't see her face. It was burning, and she suddenly felt crummy.

Here she was, about to tell Annie she was saving her money to buy a horse, when they were so worried about their business. If she was a truly good daughter, she'd offer all her earnings to them.

"Josie, I'll finish up here," Annie said. "You can go wash up, and—" she stopped.

"And what?" Josie dumped the chopped garlic into the pan of melted butter.

"Well, I was going to say you could change your clothes if you'd like." She glanced at Josie's sweatshirt, which held traces of the lasagna ingredients. "But you don't have to if you don't want to."

Annie is so nice, Josie thought. Some mothers would order their daughters to dress up when company came for dinner. Annie gave her the choice. It made her feel even worse.

"Don't let the garlic burn," she said and went out.

It seemed as if a dark, gloomy cloud had just settled on her head. Was she a rotten daughter,

36

or what? Morgan's Country Foods could be in real trouble, and all she'd been able to think about lately was that horse.

She shivered as she recalled her first look at him. He was simply beautiful, chestnut brown with a shiny coat. She remembered the way he shook his head and whinnied when she stroked him. He was the horse she'd dreamed about. Even his name was perfect – Sunshine. As she climbed the stairs, she could see herself riding him on a sunny day, his mane flapping in the warm breeze . . . but Sunshine was a horse. Annie and Ben were her parents.

Cat was coming out of the bathroom, her head wrapped in a towel. "How was your old-lady-sitting today?"

"Don't call her that," Josie snapped. "She's a senior citizen, not an old lady."

She expected Cat to respond with a sharp retort. Instead, she just shrugged and mumbled, "Okay, okay. Sorry." Her face was despondent.

Was she worried about the store, too? Josie wondered. Curious, she followed Cat into her room. "What's your problem?"

Cat flopped down on her bed and raised a mournful face. "Remember that ad I showed you? The beautiful dress at Danielle's Boutique?"

"Yeah, why?"

"I put it aside on credit. I figured I'd find a job fast and have enough money to pay it off in three weeks. But it's been *days*, and I still haven't found anything."

"Have you tried?"

"Sure I have! I went to every store in town and asked them if they wanted a model. But nobody's interested."

"I don't think there's a big demand for models in Green Falls," Josie commented. "What happens if you don't pay for the dress in time?"

"They keep my down payment. And I don't get the dress." Cat cocked her head to one side and looked at Josie thoughtfully. "You must be making a lot of money, working for that old – uh, that senior citizen."

Josie's eyes narrowed. "What about it?"

"You could give – I mean, *lend* me the money to pay for my dress."

"How would you pay me back?"

"Out of my allowance. I could give you a little each week."

Josie uttered a short laugh. "That would take forever! Besides, if business at Morgan's Country Foods doesn't improve, we may not even be getting allowances." She paused. "I've been thinking . . . maybe I should give Annie and Ben the money I'm making. To help out."

Cat shook her head. "They'd never accept it."

She's right, Josie thought. Annie and Ben wouldn't take money from their daughters.

"But *I* would," Cat said. "So you might as well lend some to me."

"I can't," Josie said. "I'm saving it."

"For what?"

"That horse I saw advertised in the newspaper."

Cat stared at her for a second. Then she fell back on her bed. "A horse? You're going to spend all that money on a dumb horse?"

Josie hadn't expected her to understand. "Look, it'll take me eight weeks to save the money for the horse. After that, I can lend you some."

"It'll be too late!" Cat wailed.

"Then . . . I'm sorry." Josie left and went to her own room. Peering into her closet, she sighed. Then she pulled out a dress. It wouldn't kill her.

Cat hit the button on the blow dryer and aimed it at her hair. A horse. Her sister was making tons of money, and she was going to blow it all on a stupid horse. What a waste. And the most beautiful dress in the world was just waiting for Cat at Danielle's Boutique.

It wasn't fair. If she could just get a job, she'd have her dress.

To cheer herself up, she envisioned Heather

39

going into Danielle's Boutique, her purse crammed with money and credit cards, and asking to see that particular dress in size five. The saleslady would tell her the only size five had been reserved. Maybe she'd tell Heather *who* had reserved it.

A satisfied smile crossed Cat's face as she pictured Heather's furious expression. Or maybe it would be even better if the saleslady didn't tell Heather, and Heather wouldn't find out until Cat walked into the Turnaround.

Her smile faded. It wasn't going to happen. Not unless she figured out a way to come up with sixty-seven dollars and fifty cents.

She didn't bother to put on any make-up. It was only a couple of friends of Annie and Ben's coming over. She slipped into some corduroy pants and a shirt and went downstairs.

"Do you need any help?" she asked as she came into the dining room.

Annie placed a pair of candlesticks in the centre of the table. "I think we're all set, Cat." She disappeared back into the kitchen.

Becka smiled at Cat. "Funny how you always manage to show up just when everything's done."

Cat looked at the table. "Becka, knives go on the *right* side of the plate, forks on the left."

"Then you can switch them around," Becka replied.

Cat slumped down into a chair, put her elbows on the table, and rested her chin in her hands. "Who are these people coming for dinner?"

"Sally and George Layton. Ben and Annie knew them back in New York. They bought the old Green Falls Inn, and Ben says they've fixed it up really nice."

Cat looked up. "They're re-opening the old inn?" With Becka's nod, an idea sprang into her head. "I'll be right back." She ran out, ignoring Becka's cry of, "Hey, what about the knives and forks?"

So the Laytons are opening the old inn, Cat thought. They'd need people to work there. There must be something she could do, like . . . like what? Then it hit her. She could be the receptionist! She saw herself wearing a nice dress, greeting guests, registering the wealthy people who came to ski in Vermont. It was the perfect job for her!

Up in her room, she began to apply make-up. Not a lot, just enough to look a little older, more sophisticated. She twisted her hair into a chic knot. Then she pulled off her clothes and threw on a simple shirtwaist dress.

Just as she slipped her feet into neat flats, the doorbell rang. Josie raced past Cat's door. Cat wasn't going to run. She wanted to make an entrance.

She waited until she heard a chorus of voices

in the living room. Then she proceeded, slowly and gracefully, down the stairs.

"And here comes our third daughter, Catherine, better known as Cat," Ben said.

"How do you do?" Cat asked. She extended a hand, first to the woman, then to the man, and smiled. "It's a pleasure to meet you. Welcome to Green Falls!"

Behind Annie's back, she could see Josie rolling her eyes. Becka had a hand over her mouth, like she was trying to stiffle giggles. Cat didn't care. She could tell from the couple's faces that she was definitely making an impression.

"I can't believe you've got three daughters," George Layton said later as they all moved into the dining room.

"You're very lucky," Sally said.

"We know," Annie joined in as she carried a steaming pan of lasagna out of the kitchen. "They bring us a lot of joy."

"And an occasional nervous breakdown," Ben added with a smile.

Cat stiffened. She hoped he wasn't about to start telling stories – like about the time she'd sneaked out of the house to go to a nightclub.

But she should have known Ben wouldn't betray family secrets. "Annie's right," he said. "Having a family has been the best thing that's ever happened to us."

"And how's your store doing?" George asked.

Annie and Ben exchanged looks. "It has its ups and downs," Ben said.

"It's going to be more up from now on," Becka reminded him. "Do you have the ad ready for me? The deadline's tomorrow."

Ben groaned. "I knew there was something I was supposed to do."

Becka sighed. "How about if I write it for you?"

"Be my guest," Ben said. He turned to the Laytons. "Becka's the writer in the family. She works on her school newspaper. And you should see the essays she does for her English class."

"Josie's our athlete," Annie told them. "She was the first girl to get into her school's basketball team."

"Wonderful!" Sally exclaimed. "By the way, this lasagna's delicious. When did you learn to cook like this? I didn't think you two even knew where the kitchen was in your apartment back in New York."

Annie laughed. "I've been learning, but I can't take credit for this. Josie made it."

"You've certainly got some talented daughters," George remarked.

Before anyone could ask Cat what *her* speciality was, she broke in. "I understand you're re-opening the Green Falls Inn."

Sally nodded. "The day after tomorrow."

"Becka's right about advertising," George

said. "We took one small ad in a Boston newspaper, and we've already got reservations coming in."

"What did you say in your ad?" Becka asked him.

"Oh, we just described the inn, how charming and quiet it is, and how close to the ski slopes." He winked at Ben. "I didn't exaggerate too much."

"George and I worked at the same advertising agency in New York," Ben explained to the others. "There were times when we were forced to exaggerate to come up with a halfway decent ad." He shook his head ruefully.

Cat spoke casually. "I suppose you're hiring people to work there."

"That's what I've been doing all day," Sally said. "Interviewing people."

"Do you have everyone you need?" Cat turned to Annie and Ben. "After hearing Josie talk about her job, I think I'd like one, too."

She couldn't blame Annie and Ben for being startled. Cat had never been known for her willingness to work.

But the Laytons were looking at her with interest. "We could always use another pair of hands," George said. "If it's all right with your parents."

Annie and Ben looked at each other. "Well,

I suppose it's okay," Annie said. "If it's not too many hours."

"Why don't you come by the inn tomorrow after school and we'll talk about it," Sally suggested.

Cat was dying to ask how much money they'd pay her. But that would have to wait. She wouldn't want them to think she was *greedy*.

Becka scrutinised her face in the bathroom mirror. The birthmark was still there. Was it a little lighter, maybe? No, she couldn't honestly say she saw any difference in it at all. Josie was right. The ad had lied.

Becka went back to her bedroom and shut the door. Then she sat down at her desk, turned on the desk lamp, and began chewing on a pencil.

Morgan's Country Foods. What could she say about Morgan's Country Foods that would make people want to buy stuff there? She thought about the ads she'd seen in newspapers and magazines, the commercials she'd watched on television. They all made wonderful promises and guarantees. That's what got people to buy the products. They exaggerated, according to Ben and George. If *Invisicream* was any example, they lied, too.

She thought for a while. Her creative juices started to flow, and she began to write.

Four

The next day, Cat left her class and hurried to her locker. She didn't want to be late for her meeting with the Laytons at the inn.

"Uh, hi, Cat." Todd, her ex-boyfriend, was standing by his locker. Out of the corner of her eye, Cat could see the lopsided grin that used to make her heart flutter. She glanced at him briefly, just to let him know she'd heard him. Then she breezed past him without speaking.

She caught a flash of his crestfallen face. *Serves him right,* she thought. Still, memories flooded her mind. Football games, movies, Luigi's for pizza. For a second, she almost felt wistful. Then she recalled that it was *always* football games, movies, Luigi's for pizza. Boring. Even so, she would have liked to have been the one who dumped him, not the other way around. And to be dumped for Heather Beaumont. The thought still rankled.

Cat reached her locker and started turning the combination. A group of boys passed, reminding her that she still had to figure out who to ask to the Turnaround. Now that she knew she was actually going to get that dress, she could get excited about the dance. If only she could think of a guy worth wearing it for. . . .

She opened the locker. Just as she was putting on her coat, she saw Britt and Marla running down the hall.

"I'm so glad we caught you," Marla said breathlessly.

"We were afraid you'd already left," Britt gasped.

"What's up?" Cat asked, eyeing them curiously.

Britt's face was flushed with excitement. "Wait till you hear what we found out!"

"Britt was in the bathroom," Marla began, "and—"

"Oh, let me tell it," Britt pleaded.

"Somebody tell me!" Cat demanded. "And quick! I have to get to the inn."

Britt took a deep breath. "I'd just come out of study hall, last period. I went into the rest room. You know, the one by the media centre, near the water fountain . . ."

"Yes, yes, I know," Cat said impatiently.

"Anyway, I went into one of the stalls. And guess who came in?"

"Britt, just tell her," Marla ordered.

"Heather and Blair Chase. Honestly, that Blair is such a dork. She tags after Heather like—"

47

"Britt!" Cat and Marla shrieked in unison.

"Okay, okay. I heard Blair ask Heather if she was going to take Todd to the Turnaround. And Heather said no, she broke up with him."

"Is that all?" Cat slammed her locker shut. "I told you, there's no way I'm asking Todd. Besides, I wouldn't want Heather's rejects."

"Wait, she hasn't gotten to the good part," Marla said. "Britt *tell* her."

"So Blair asked Heather who she *was* going to ask. And Heather said – are you ready for this?"

Frustrated, Marla finished for her. "She wants to ask Sid Belcher."

Cat's mouth fell open. "Sid Belcher! Britt, are you sure she said Sid Belcher?" When Britt nodded, Cat shook her head in disbelief. "No way."

"There's nothing wrong with my hearing. She said it loud and clear." Britt's forehead puckered. "Funny, Heather's usually so secretive about who she likes. And they must have known I was in there. They were right behind me in the hall. Kind of strange, don't you think?"

"What's really strange is Heather Beaumont asking Sid Belcher to the Turnaround," Cat said. "Why would she ever be interested in a greaser?"

Marla considered that. "Well, he's sort of

interesting looking. If you like the type."

Cat made a face. She simply could not picture Heather with a boy who wore a skull and crossbones earring and sweatshirts with the sleeves cut off to display his tattoo. Privately, Cat suspected it wasn't a real tattoo. But it didn't matter. It still looked gross.

"Very weird," Cat murmured. "Look, I've got to go."

Marla and Britt walked along with her. "So what are you going to do?" Marla asked.

"About what?"

"Remember the other day when you said you'd like to find out who Heather was going to ask to the dance so you could ask him first?"

Cat was aghast. "Marla, you're not saying I should ask Sid Belcher!"

"You have to admit, it would be a great way to get even with her," Britt said.

"Are you nuts? Forget it!"

"You could ask him now and then break the date right before the dance," Marla suggested.

Cat wrinkled her nose. "That's an awfully mean thing to do. Even to a greaser."

"Yeah, I guess you're right," Marla said.

Cat sighed. "Too bad she isn't planning to ask someone more, more . . ."

"Human?" Marla asked.

"Right. See ya later." Cat left the building and began walking rapidly. She'd told Sally

49

Layton she'd be at the inn at three-thirty, and it was past that now. She wasn't really worried, though. After all, the Laytons were friends of her parents. She'd get the job whether or not she was on time.

As she walked, she considered the news she'd just heard. Heather with Sid Belcher . . . never in a million years would she have put those two together. Heather was so into being cool. Sid was the kind of person who smoked cigarettes in the boys' room and got suspended. Totally uncool.

It was too bad. It would have been fun to snag the boy Heather liked – but no way was she going after Sid. At least Cat would have the dress Heather wanted. That was something.

The Laytons had done a terrific job with the inn, Cat thought as she approached it. The last time she'd seen the building, its outside was peeling, windows were broken, and it looked generally rundown.

Now it gleamed and shined and looked positively elegant. If she had to work, this was a nice place to do it, Cat decided happily. She turned the brass knob on the front door and walked inside.

The lobby area was lovely, full of antique furniture, including a grandfather clock. Two flowered sofas faced each other, with a pretty rug between them. The reception desk was polished wood, with an old-fashioned telephone on it. Cat could see herself standing behind it, greeting guests, answering the phone.

What she didn't see was any sign of the Laytons. Of course, the inn wasn't scheduled to open until tomorrow, but Sally or George had to be around somewhere. "Hello?" Cat called. When there was no response, she slipped off her coat, sat down on one of the sofas, and picked up a magazine from the coffee table.

"What are you doing?"

Cat turned her head in the direction of the harsh voice. A woman with a face like a prune stood there.

Cat smiled brightly. "Is Sally Layton around?"

"Who wants to see her?"

"I'm Cat Morgan."

The woman nodded shortly, as if she recognized the name. But it didn't change her sour expression. "They told me you'd be coming at three-thirty. It's now four o'clock. I will not tolerate tardiness."

Cat stared at her in bewilderment. What was it to her if Cat was a little late? "I'm supposed to see Sally Layton about a job here."

The woman sniffed. "You're seeing me."

"Um, excuse me, but who are you?"

"I'm Miss Andrews, the housekeeper." She surveyed Cat and shook her head. "You don't look like you're going to be much of a maid."

Cat couldn't have heard correctly. "Did you say – a maid?"

"What size dress do you wear?"

Dazed, Cat managed to mumble, "Size five. Why do you want to know?"

"For your uniform, of course."

"Uniform?" Cat asked faintly.

"Your hours are three-thirty to five-thirty, Monday, Wednesday and Friday. You will report to me. As I said, you must be on time."

Cat swallowed. "What – what exactly will I be doing?"

Miss Andrews gave a look that clearly indicated her opinion of Cat. "What do you think a maid does? You'll sweep, dust, mop . . ."

The horrid words continued to come, but Cat wasn't hearing them anymore. She was in a state of shock.

"Your move," Mrs Daley barked.

Josie contemplated the chequerboard. She saw a place she could move to where Mrs Daley could jump her. Should she do it? No, Mrs Daley wasn't some little kid she had to go easy on. She'd want to win only if she could do it on her own. Josie moved her chequer somewhere else.

Mrs Daley's face was expressionless. Then the corners of her lips twitched. She picked up a chequer, jumped Josie's three remaining ones, and won the game.

"I didn't see that!" Josie wailed as Mrs Daley threw back her head and laughed.

"You're going to have to open your eyes if you want to beat me, child!"

"How did you learn to play chequers so well?" Josie asked.

"Many years ago, when I was skiing in the Swiss Alps, I broke my leg," Mrs Daley said. "Laid me up for a month. So I mastered every game I could get my hands on." She shook a finger at Josie. "For your own sake, never invite me into a game of poker."

"You've been everywhere, haven't you?"

"Just about, my dear. Never got to go to college, though. In my day, some parents didn't believe in education for a girl. But travel is a great education in itself."

"Of all the places you've travelled to, what was your favourite?" Josie asked.

Mrs Daley shook her head. "I don't believe in having favourites. There's something good to be said for every place I've been. Just like there's something good about every person I've known."

"I love hearing you describe your travels," Josie told her. "You make countries sound so much more interesting than my geography teacher at school."

"There are photos from some of my trips over there on that table," Mrs Daley said.

Josie had noticed the huge collection of framed photos on the corner table, but she hadn't examined them. She didn't want Mrs Daley to think she was nosy. But now that she had permission to look, she went over to the table.

"Wow, where's this old building? It looks like it's hundreds of years old."

Mrs Daley squinted. "Bring it closer, Josie." When Josie did, she scrutinised the photo. "Try more than a thousand years. That's the Forum, in Rome."

Josie put the photo back. There were so many interesting looking ones, she didn't know which to ask Mrs Daley about next. Snow-capped mountains, beautiful lakes, forests, castles, Heather Beaumont – Josie stopped. What was a photo of Heather Beaumont doing here?

"What are you looking at now?" Mrs Daley demanded, peering at her.

Josie brought the photo over to her. "Isn't this Heather Beaumont?"

"You know her?" Mrs Daley asked.

"Sure. She's in my class at school."

Mrs Daley nodded. "That's right. She would be in the eighth grade now."

"Why do you have a picture of her?"

"She's my granddaughter."

"Heather Beaumont is your *granddaughter?*"

"Something wrong with your hearing? That's what I said. Why do you look so surprised?"

"I don't know. I guess because you never mentioned having a granddaughter."

Mrs Daley grunted. "Maybe that's because sometimes I forget I have one."

Josie looked at her sceptically. There was nothing wrong with this woman's mind.

Mrs Daley grinned. "I don't mean that literally. She just doesn't come around to visit much. Only when her mother, my daughter, makes her."

How could a neat person like Mrs Daley be related to someone as creepy and snobby and mean as Heather Beaumont? "That's terrible," Josie stated. "If I had a grandmother, I'd visit her all the time."

"You don't have any grandparents?"

Josie shook her head, and Mrs Daley eyed her keenly. "Child, I don't know much about you. I'm always telling you stories about myself, but I haven't heard any stories from you. Tell me about yourself."

Josie busied herself putting photos back the way they were. "There's not much to tell."

"Nonsense," Mrs Daley stated. "Everyone's got a story. I want to hear yours." She rapped her cane on the floor. "Come here."

It was a direct order. Reluctantly, Josie left

the table and sat down in a chair across from the woman. "My life's not very interesting," she said.

"I'll decide what's interesting and what's not. I'm the boss here. I pay your salary, right? Well, okay, my son-in-law does. In any case, I'm in charge and I want to know about you. Start talking."

Josie had to smile. There was something about Mrs Daley that reminded her so much of Mrs Parker, the cook back at Willoughby Hall who had been Josie's closest friend. Like Mrs Parker, Mrs Daley was gruff on the outside but warm and kind on the inside. They were both real, no-nonsense, down-to-earth people.

Josie had the feeling she could trust Mrs Daley the way she had trusted Mrs Parker. So she started to talk.

"I was born in Texas." That was easy. Now came the hard part. "My parents were killed in a car accident when I was five." She tried to speak matter-of-factly, but she choked a little. Clenching her fists, she waited for the automatic look of pity she'd seen so many times to appear on Mrs Daley's face. But it didn't come.

Josie relaxed. She should have known. Mrs Parker never gave her those awfuly pitying looks either.

"Go on," the elderly woman said.

"I was sent to live with a cousin in Vermont.

But she – she had her own kids and she didn't really want me. I went to some foster homes, but they didn't work out. So I was put in an orphanage. Willoughby Hall."

"How long were you there?"

"Till last July. I was adopted, by Annie and Ben Morgan. We live on Church Road. Our store, Morgan's Country Foods, is right across the street."

"I believe I met them when they first moved to Green Falls," Mrs Daley said. "So the Morgans adopted a thirteen-year-old girl? They're brave people."

Josie grinned. "They adopted *three* thirteen-year-old girls." She told Mrs Daley about Cat and Becka. Before long, she found herself telling Mrs Daley all about their experiences back at Willoughby Hall, and their life for the past five months with the Morgans.

Mrs Daley was a great listener, nodding, laughing, exclaiming at all the right times. "If your parents have a store, how come you're working here?"

"I needed to make some money. You see, I want to buy a horse."

"Aha! I knew it!"

"You knew what?"

"I just knew you'd be a horse lover." Her eyes became soft. "When I was your age, you couldn't drag me off my horse. A person would have thought there was glue on the seat of my riding britches."

Josie nodded fervently. "That's how I'm going to be. What was your horse's name?"

"Moonlight."

"Hey, that's sort of a coincidence! The horse I want to buy is called Sunshine."

"How much does this Sunshine cost?"

"Four hundred dollars. I figure I'll have enough saved up in eight weeks."

"I see." Mrs Daley was quiet for a minute. "You plan to quit coming here then?"

"Oh no!" Josie exclaimed. "I'm going to have to go on making money to keep him. I haven't told my parents about Sunshine yet, but I'm going to be responsible for him. I have to feed him, and I want to buy a good saddle, and some riding boots. Besides . . . I *like* coming here."

Mrs Daley beamed at her. "And I like having you here. Now, is the owner of Sunshine going to hold on to him until you have the money?"

"Not exactly. He said if he gets another buyer before then, he'll have to sell him. But no one's come to see the horse besides me. I'm just hoping no one will before I get all the money saved up."

"Sounds to me like you're taking a risk. Look, I've got a little money put aside. How about if I lend you the four hundred dollars now?"

Josie breathed in sharply. What a great friend Mrs Daley was! To be able to buy Sunshine right now, today maybe, and not have to worry that someone else would buy him first . . . it was so tempting.

But she shook her head. It wasn't right. Annie and Ben wouldn't approve of her borrowing the money. And she wouldn't feel good about it herself.

"Thanks a lot, but I think I'd better wait until I earn it."

She saw approval in Mrs Daley's eyes. "I can't say I blame you. Something always seems more yours when you pay for it with your own hard-earned money."

Josie grinned. "Except that it hasn't been very hard earning *this* money."

Mrs Daley's eyebrows shot up. "Oh, no? Hmm . . ." She looked around the room. "Seems to me those windows are getting a little dirty."

They both started laughing.

Five

The *Green Gazette* arrived from the printer every Monday just as school was letting out. Becka, like most students, usually waited until Tuesday morning to pick up her copy and read it in homeroom. But this particular Monday, she waited impatiently just outside the school entrance for its arrival.

Finally, the car bearing the words GREEN FALLS PRINT SHOP pulled up in front of the school. A man jumped out, carrying a stack of newspapers tied with twine in each hand. Becka followed him into the school.

The man had barely finished cutting the twine before Becka grabbed the first copy. She disregarded the articles and news, and went directly to the back of the newspaper where the ads were. Her eyes scanned the page. Sports Stuff, The Town Shoppe . . . there it was!

She read the words she'd written with pride. In all modesty, she had to say it was a very creative ad. If this didn't help business, nothing would.

She felt very good about herself. Cat was

working for a dress, Josie was working for a horse. Only Becka was working to help her family. Ben and Annie would be so happy.

As she re-read the ad, savouring each and every word, two girls she didn't know picked up copies of the newspaper. She didn't pay any attention until she heard one of them say to the other, "Hey, did you see this ad?"

"Wow," the other one replied. "That's amazing."

Becka couldn't resist. "Which ad are you talking about?"

"Morgan's Country Foods," the first girl told her. "Look what it says about their maple syrup!"

Becka made a big show of widening her eyes and raising her eyebrows. "My goodness! That's remarkable!"

As the girls walked away, she overheard the other one saying, "I'm going to show this to my mother." Becka wanted to jump for joy. It was going to work! She saw Cat coming towards the exit and ran to her.

"Cat! Look at my ad!" She thrust the paper in Cat's face. Cat pushed it away.

"Not now, Becka." With her head down, she stalked out the door.

Becka gazed after her in mild curiosity. What was the matter with *her*?

Cat walked at a steadfast pace, her face set

in a grim expression. Glancing at her watch, she quickened her step. She knew what Miss Andrews' reaction would be if she was late. This was only Cat's second real working day at the Green Falls Inn. She wished it was her last.

Her thoughts went back to Friday. It had been a disaster. She couldn't do anything right, at least, not according to Miss Andrews. Cat left streaks on the windows, she didn't sweep properly, and she broke one of the stupid china figurines on the lobby mantle while she was dusting. For two hours, Miss Andrews had hovered over her, scolding and snapping and complaining. Well, what did she expect? Cat Morgan was *not* cut out to be a maid.

Somehow, she'd managed to keep up a brave front at home over the weekend. She couldn't very well let Ben and Annie know how miserable she was, not when she was working for their friends. Even thinking about her new dress didn't bring much comfort, considering what she was going through to get it.

In Cat's eyes, the Green Falls Inn no longer looked pretty and quaint. It was beginning to resemble a torture chamber. With extreme reluctance, she opened the door and went in.

From the lobby, Cat could see into the dining room. Guests were sitting at tables, having afternoon tea. Conversation and laughter drifted out into the lobby. Cat felt even more sorry for herself.

"Morgan!"

Cat flinched. "Yes, Miss Andrews?"

"What are you waiting for? Get into your uniform immediately."

Cat went into the little bathroom behind the reception desk and took off her skirt and sweater. Then, with a grimace, she slipped into her uniform and tied the apron around her waist. She tried to avoid the mirror, but habit forced her eyes automatically in that direction.

For once, she didn't smile and preen at the image she saw. Her reflection revolted her. Grey had to be her very worst colour. It made her skin look yellow. The uniform was baggy and shapeless. And that wretched apron! It was a sign, telling the whole world she was a maid.

Scowling, she pulled her hair back in an elastic band, the way Miss Andrews insisted she wear it. One lock refused to be gathered and fell down the side of her face.

I look like Cinderella, Cat thought. *Before* the visit from her fairy godmother. She could only be grateful that all the guests were from out of town, and she wasn't likely ever to see any of them again.

Emerging from the room, she passed Sally Layton behind the reception desk. The woman gave her a slightly anxious smile. "Hello, Cat. How is everything working out?"

Cat forced a return smile. "Just fine."

"Good, good. Miss Andrews, I'll be in the dining room if anyone wants me."

Miss Andrews' piercing eyes hit Cat. "Follow me." She led Cat to a storage closet, where she took out a can of furniture polish and a nasty-looking rag. "Do the banister."

Cat took the rag gingerly between two fingers and went to the stairs. The ornate carved railing along its side looked perfectly fine to her. But Miss Andrews was standing there, so Cat poured a little polish on the rag and stroked the wood.

"Not like that!" Miss Andrews barked. "Put some elbow grease into it!"

Elbow grease. What a disgusting expression. Cat polished a little faster.

Miss Andrews snatched the rag out of her hands. "Like this!" She rubbed the railing vigorously. "Haven't you ever polished furniture before?" She snorted. "Are you afraid of ruining your nails?"

Cat pressed her lips together tightly. *Don't say it, Cat,* she warned herself.

"Just what I need," the housekeeper muttered. "Some little pampered princess working here."

A rush of conflicting emotions battled inside

64

Cat. On the one hand, she wanted to inform this witch that she had lived in an orphanage for thirteen years and had done her share of drudgery. Not to mention the fact that she had regular chores at home. On the other hand, she rather liked having the image of a pampered princess.

"Are you listening to me?" Miss Andrews asked.

Are you saying anything worth listening to? Cat wanted to ask. She quickly drummed up a mental picture of her dress and replied, "Yes, ma'am."

"Then get to work."

Cat rubbed until the housekeeper left the area. Then she examined her hands. They were covered with brown streaks. Gook was collecting under her fingernails. The polish on one nail was chipped.

Waves of self-pity engulfed her. She felt like she was back at Willoughby Hall, a poor, neglected orphan, slaving away. Okay, she hadn't been neglected at Willoughby Hall, and no one ever treated her like a slave. The Green Falls Inn was definitely worse than an orphanage.

Two women came down the stairs and stepped past her as if she was invisible. Well, who *would* notice a maid? Oh, the shame of it all. . . .

Step by step, Cat mounted the stairs, dragging the rag up the banister. Thank goodness her friends couldn't see her now. Her lunchmates knew she was working here, but she'd managed to avoid telling them exactly what she was doing. Her reputation would be in shreds.

Finally, she reached the top. Then she stepped back down, looking at the banister as she went. It didn't look any different to her.

Miss Andrews was nowhere in sight. Thankfully, Cat collapsed on the bottom stair. Through the railing, she watched as the door to the inn opened. A man and a woman, both carrying suitcases, entered.

"This is charming," the woman exclaimed.

"A real New England inn," the man said.

Cat glanced at them with disinterest. Then she saw a boy, also carrying suitcases, come in after them.

He looked about her age, not very tall, but absolutely *adorable*. His hair was so blond it was practically white. And he had a tan – something unheard-of at this time of the year in Vermont.

Sally Layton bustled out of the dining room. "You must be the Hudsons."

The man put down his suitcase and shook hands with her. "Howard and Joan. And this is our son, Bailey."

Bailey, Cat mused. *What a neat name.*

"Welcome to the Green Falls Inn. If you'll come sign in over here, I'll show you to your rooms."

As Sally led them to the desk, Cat moved back slightly, but it was too late. Sally saw her sitting there, and she frowned slightly. "Uh, Cat, maybe you could help with the luggage."

Cat rose and went over to them.

"Take this one up to room four," Sally said, pointing to one.

Cat was aware of the boy's eyes on her. She was in agony, thinking of how she must look. She grabbed the suitcase and started back up the stairs. She was almost halfway up when she heard footsteps behind her.

"Here, let me take that."

The fair-haired boy took the suitcase from her hand. "If you'll just show me where my room is . . ."

With her head down, Cat hurried up the rest of the stairs. Once on the landing, she pointed towards the room. But he didn't move.

"My name's Bailey Hudson."

For a moment, Cat was taken aback. It was the first time a guest of the inn had spoken directly to her. Bailey had a nice smile, not crooked like Todd's but full and wide and showing even white teeth. Under normal circumstances, Cat would know exactly how to behave when meeting a really cute guy for the first time. But how could she flirt when she was dressed like a maid?

"And your name's Cat. I heard the lady downstairs call you that. I've never known anyone with that name."

Cat found her power of speech. "It's really Catherine. Catherine Morgan. Cat's a nickname."

"Oh. It's neat." He glanced towards the window at the end of the hall. "You know, this is the first time I've ever seen real snow. I'm from California."

"Wow. I've never been there. I've never been out of Vermont."

"California's pretty cool. It's sunny most of the time, and it's a great place for surfing. But it must be nice living in a place that has four seasons."

Cat listened in awe. Most of the boys she knew could barely string two sentences together.

"Morgan!"

Miss Andrews seemed to have materialised out of nowhere. "Cat! Don't bother the guests," she hissed. "You have work to do. Come downstairs."

"Excuse me," Cat mumbled, her face hot and burning with embarrassment. She turned away from Bailey and followed the housekeeper back downstairs, passing the Hudsons and Sally Layton on their way up. Back in the lobby, Miss

Andrews handed her another rag and pointed.

"Dust," she commanded.

Once again, Cat felt like Cinderella, only now she'd just met the prince. Too bad he was just visiting. But maybe that was for the best. He couldn't like her, knowing she was a maid.

Why weren't there cute, interesting guys like that at school? In frustration, Cat slapped the rag at the table. It hit the rim of a bowl of candy and the bowl tipped over, spilling candy all over the floor.

Miss Andrews magically appeared again. "What happened?"

"The bowl tipped over."

"All by itself?" The woman folded her arms. "What are you waiting for *this* time? Pick it up!"

Cat got down on her hands and knees and began picking up the candies. She had to crawl under the table to reach them all. Suddenly, a gust of cold air told her the front door had opened. She heard Sally Layton saying, "Good afternoon. May I help you?" A woman's voice replied, "Yes, we're meeting the Hudsons for tea. Have they arrived?"

"I'll call their room," Sally said. "Could I have your name, please?"

"Mrs Beaumont."

As in *Heather's mother?* Cat wondered. Cat turned her head to get a look. A tall woman with streaked blonde hair, wearing a mink coat, stood there. She wasn't alone. Cat swallowed and almost choked. Standing beside Mrs Beaumont was Heather.

Still on her hands and knees, Cat edged backward, praying that Heather wouldn't look down. This couldn't, *couldn't* be happening to her. Sally Layton put down the telephone and returned to the Beaumonts.

"The Hudsons are coming right down. Won't you have a seat?" To Cat's horror, Sally led them to the twin sofas. Sitting there, Heather would have to see her.

For once, Cat had a little luck. Just as Heather and her mother started following Sally, a voice trilled from the stairs. "Gloria! How lovely to see you again!"

From her hiding place, Cat could see Mrs Hudson and Bailey join the Beaumonts, and she heard Mrs Hudson introduce Bailey to Heather. Cat gritted her teeth as she watched Heather toss her head so her blonde curls bounced on her shoulders.

Thankfully, they all moved into the dining room, and Cat relaxed slightly. She didn't get to stay that way for long.

"What are you still doing there?" Miss Andrews said.

Sally Layton turned, and for the first time saw Cat under the table.

"Uh, just getting the last pieces," Cat said.

"How long does it take you to pick up candy?"

Cat had no answer for that. She quickly picked up the remaining ones. Emerging from her cave, she stood up and noticed with resignation that the front of her uniform was smudged with dust. She hoped the housekeeper wouldn't see it. Cat was supposed to have swept under there on Friday, but she had figured no one would notice if she didn't.

Miss Andrews was deep in conversation with Sally Layton. Their backs were to Cat, but Sally turned slightly and cast a worried look in her direction. She quickly averted her eyes when she realised Cat was watching. Cat had a pretty good idea who they were talking about.

She emptied the candies in a wastebasket and made a few ineffectual swipes at the front of her uniform. She looked at the grandfather clock in the corner and stifled a groan. Forty-five minutes left. With one nervous eye on the entrance to the dining room, Cat approached Miss Andrews. "What would you like me to do now?"

Miss Andrews and Sally exchanged looks. Miss Andrews sighed. "Go upstairs and . . . and look in the rooms. Check to see if there are fresh flowers in the vases."

"You can put in more water if they need it," Sally said.

"But *try* not to spill it," the housekeeper added. She handed Cat the master key.

What a relief. At least this would put her out of the general vicinity of the dining room, and Heather Beaumont.

When Cat reached the top of the stairs, she leaned against the wall and closed her eyes. Heather Beaumont. Of all the people she didn't want to run into. If she hadn't been under that table, Heather would have seen her. It was too unbelievably gruesome to think about.

Now, if she could just dawdle up here till Heather left . . . Cat started moving very, very slowly. She went to the first door, unlocked it, and went in. She checked the two vases and pulled out a few limp flowers.

Then she went to the next room and did the same. In the third room, she added some water to the vases. No one was staying in there, so she spent a few moments poking around, looking at the pictures on the wall, admiring the fancy soaps in the bathroom, and feeling the thick, plush towels.

She was unlocking the door to the next room when she heard voices on the stairway.

"How big is the junior high? How many students?" Cat recognised Bailey's voice.

"I don't know. I never counted." That was followed by an all-too-familiar tinkling laugh.

Frantically, Cat turned the key, scurried into

the room, and closed the door. She was about to allow herself a sigh of relief when she heard a key in the lock!

Cat ducked into the bathroom and pulled the door closed. A second later she heard Bailey's voice. "Gee, I thought I'd locked it. This is my room."

Wildly, Cat wondered if they could hear her heart pounding through the bathroom door. It certainly sounded loud enough to her.

"It's nice," Heather replied. "I mean, for a little place like this. Of course, it's nothing like the hotel we stay in when we go to New York. That place is like a palace. Our rooms there are twice this size."

"This rooms suits me okay," came Bailey's easy reply.

"How long will you be staying here?"

"Just till our house is finished being painted. Friday or Saturday. That's when the movers are supposed to arrive from California."

"When will you start coming to school?"

"Next Monday, after we get settled in."

It took a few moments for the significance of his words to penetrate Cat's panic. When they did, she wanted to sink to the floor. This boy, this adorable Bailey Hudson, wasn't visiting Green Falls. He was *moving* to Green Falls. Next week, he'd be at Green Falls Junior High. She'd see him, in the halls, in the cafeteria, maybe in a class or two. He'd say, "Didn't I see you working as a maid at the Green Falls Inn?" Other kids would hear him.

But she had someone else to worry about first. "What are the bathrooms like here?" Heather asked.

"Like ordinary bathrooms," Bailey replied.

"Could I see it? I'd like to brush my hair."

Cat was momentarily paralysed. But her finely tuned instincts took over. She whipped off her apron and stuffed it under the sink. Just as the doorknob started to turn, she grabbed it and pushed.

Heather almost toppled over. Cat wasn't sure if it was from being pushed by the door or from the shock of seeing Cat come out of Bailey's bathroom.

Heather recovered quickly. "What are *you* doing here?"

Think, Cat ordered herself. *Think!* She laughed lightly to give herself time. "Why, Heather, what a surprise. The owners here are friends of my parents. They invited me over to see the new inn."

Heather wasn't completely satisfied. "What are you doing in *this* room?"

"Well, if it's any of your business, I thought it was empty." She turned to Bailey. "I'm very sorry." With her eyes, she tried to communicate a message: *Please don't tell! Don't let her know*

I'm a maid! It was so hopeless. How could she expect him to figure out what she was thinking? He didn't even know her!

Bailey was watching them both with interest, his eyes darting back and forth between them. Then that big smile appeared. "Like I said, I guess I forgot to lock the door."

Luckily, Heather was still so startled by Cat's appearance that she didn't seem to notice the awful grey dress. But given more time, Cat knew she would.

"Excuse me," Cat said. She brushed past Heather and sauntered out, closing the door behind her. Her hands were shaking as she fumbled with the key and went into the room next door. How many close calls could a person have in one day?

She pressed her head against the door. A few seconds later, a faint voice drifted up from somewhere downstairs. "Heather!" Then she heard Bailey's door open.

"Coming, Mother. It was nice meeting you, Bailey. Maybe we can get together after school later this week."

Cat couldn't hear Bailey's reply. But she could imagine it. She'd seen Heather's effect on boys at school when she turned on the charm.

What a crummy break, Cat thought. Cute boys were not a dime a dozen at Green Falls Junior High. Bailey would definitely be welcome. And

Heather had already sunk her claws into him. Oh, why couldn't Cat have met him for the first time at school, where she could have had a fighting chance?

Cat listened for Heather's footsteps on the stairs. Then she quietly opened her door and stepped out into the hall. She waited for the goodbyes. Finally, for what seemed like the first time that day, she exhaled.

Miss Andrews would be looking for her any minute now. She might as well go downstairs. She closed the door behind her, locked it, and headed down the hall.

"Cat?"

Bailey was standing outside his door, holding out an apron. Cat thought she detected a twinkle in his eyes.

"Is this yours?"

"Thank you." Cat took the apron and fled down the stairs.

Six

On Wednesday, Josie sat at lunch with her usual companions, all members of the basketball team. They were discussing the schedule of games, which would start in January. As interested as she was, Josie couldn't seem to pay attention. Her thoughts, and her eyes, kept drifting to a table on the other side of the cafeteria. There was something she wanted to do, but she didn't know if she had the guts to do it.

Observing Heather Beaumont, Josie once again experienced the feeling of disbelief she'd felt when Mrs Daley had first told her about Heather. How could a kind, funny, down-to-earth woman like Mrs Daley have such a horrible granddaughter? Horrible wasn't too strong a word for Heather. Josie could think of worse adjectives. Why, if Heather had gotten her way, Josie wouldn't even be on the basketball team.

And yet, Mrs Daley seemed to care about the girl. Just the other day, Josie had had to get something for the elderly woman from her bedroom. In there, she'd seen several framed photos of Heather at different ages.

Maybe that wasn't so surprising. Mrs Daley had to care about Heather. After all, she *was* her grandmother. But Heather didn't even bother to visit her. Josie thought that was disgusting. Even if Mrs Daley didn't show it, Josie knew she must be hurt by Heather's neglect. She hated the thought of that wonderful woman feeling bad. As much as she didn't want to do this, she felt like she owed it to Mrs Daley.

Before Josie could lose her nerve, she got up and strode purposefully across the room. When she reached Heather's table, she stopped and coughed loudly.

Heather and her two girlfriends turned towards Josie. Eve Dedham started to smile, but that little friendly gesture was stopped by Heather's sharp glance.

"What do *you* want?" Heather asked.

Josie steeled herself. "I want to talk to you about your grandmother."

She might as well have said she wanted to talk about the solar system. Heather's expression changed from contempt to utter bewilderment. "My grandmother?"

"Mrs Daley. I've been working for her, and—"

Heather interrupted. "*You've* been working for *my* grandmother?" She was beginning to sound like a parrot.

78

"Yes, just part-time." As she spoke, Josie tried to see something of Mrs Daley in Heather's face, but found nothing.

Heather had recovered her composure. "That's very interesting, Josie. Maybe you'll earn enough money to get some decent clothes."

Josie ignored the insult. "What I wanted to tell you is that I think your grandmother is lonely. It would be nice if you dropped by to see her once in a while."

Heather's pale green eyes became dangerously dark. "I don't see how that's any of your business."

"I like your grandmother," Josie replied simply. "She's my friend."

Blair, Heather's tag-along friend, sneered. "You must be pretty desperate for friends if you're hanging out with an old lady."

Josie bit her tongue to hold back a retort. She didn't want to start an argument. Besides, it wasn't her place to speak up for Mrs Daley when her own granddaughter was there.

But Heather didn't make any attempt to defend her grandmother. Her small, cold eyes were still fixed on Josie. They gave Josie the creeps.

"Hey, Heather," Blair said, "there's Sid Belcher." She started giggling like a hyena. Heather's eyes darted from Josie to Blair to the greaser who was ambling by. Then she put a hand over her heart.

"Ooh, every time I see him I get goose bumps. He is *so* incredible."

"Sid Belcher?" Josie blurted out. She took a furtive look at the boy with the slicked-back hair and torn sweatshirt. He was *awful*.

Heather turned back to Josie. "Was there anything else you wanted?"

"No." Josie walked away, shaking her head. What a waste of time that had been. She saw Cat beckoning her and went to her table.

"What were you talking to Heather about?"

"I told her she ought to visit her grand-mother."

Cat's reaction was similar to Heather's. "Her grandmother?"

"Mrs Daley. The woman I work for."

Cat's eyes widened. "Your Mrs Daley is Heather's grandmother?"

Josie could see Cat's brain clicking away. "Don't get any bright ideas. I'm not using Mrs Daley so you can get back at Heather for something." She sighed. "Heather never visits Mrs Daley. When I told her she should, all she wanted to do was giggle about some guy."

"What guy?" Marla asked.

Josie made a face. "Sid Belcher."

"See?" Marla and Britt said to Cat in unison.

"Unbelievable," Cat breathed. Her eyes

searched the cafeteria and rested on Sid Belcher, leaning against a wall with a couple of his greaser buddies. "What does she see in him?"

Before anyone could hazard a guess, Becka joined them. "Hi. Are you guys working after school?"

When both Cat and Josie nodded, Becka said, "Too bad."

"Why?" Josie asked.

"I was hoping you could help out at the store. We might get a big crowd."

"Are you kidding?" Cat asked scornfully. "There hasn't been a big crowd in there for ages."

"I know. But by now, people might have seen my ad in the *Green Gazette*. Have you heard people talking about it?"

The girls all shook their heads. "I haven't even read the *Gazette* yet," Cat said.

"Me neither." Josie looked at Becka curiously. "It's been out for two days now. Were there any more customers in the store yesterday?"

"No," Becka admitted. "Well, I guess I'll go to my locker."

"I have to go, too," Josie said. "See you later, Cat."

Cat nodded, but her eyes were still on Sid Belcher. Was there anything at all about him that was even slightly attractive? There *had* to be, if Heather was really interested in him. Cat thought maybe she should strike up a conversation with him sometime and find out what his secret appeal was. The idea didn't exactly thrill her. Another face crossed her mind. Bailey Hudson. But that was pure wishful thinking. . . .

"Is the inn really nice?" Marla asked. "Maybe we could come by and see it."

"Yeah," Britt said. "How about today?"

Cat gave them both a weak smile. "Gee, I wish you could, but, um . . . the Laytons don't like people who aren't guests coming by."

It was a pretty lame excuse. From the doubtful looks on her friends' faces, she didn't think they bought it. But thank goodness, they didn't press the subject.

When Josie arrived at Mrs Daley's that afternoon, the older woman was giving Sue Campbell a list. "Check to see if they have those little chocolate cream puffs at the bakery. Maybe you could pick up a small cake, too."

"What's going on?" Josie asked.

Mrs Daley's bright eyes were sparkling even more than usual. "My granddaughter called a few minutes ago. She's coming by for a visit!"

Josie's mouth dropped open. "Heather? She's

coming here today?" Josie was stunned. She'd only made a little suggestion to Heather, which didn't seem to have been appreciated. But she must have gotten through to her! Josie gave herself a mental pat on the back.

"And it's about time," Sue stated. "How long has it been since she last came to see you?"

"Now, now," Mrs Daley remonstrated. "Heather means well. But she's a teenager. She's got more important things on her mind than visiting an old lady."

What could be more important than visiting your own grandmother? Josie wondered. But she didn't say anything. Mrs Daley obviously didn't want to hear anything negative about Heather.

Sue left the house with the shopping list, and Mrs Daley began hobbling about, rearranging some magazines on the coffee table and plumping pillows on the sofa.

"Here, let me do that," Josie offered. "You sit down."

"You're a good girl, Josie." Mrs Daley eased herself onto the sofa. "I must admit, I'm a little tired. Ever since Heather called, I've been so excited. Sue was right. It's been a long time since I've seen her. The past few times I went to their house for dinner, she wasn't even home. I *am* looking forward to this visit."

Josie smiled. She hoped she'd be able to hold on to her smile once Heather arrived. She wasn't much of an actress. "Maybe when Heather gets here, I should leave the two of you alone," she suggested.

"Nonsense! I'm planning a real tea party, and I want you to join us."

"But you two will have so much to catch up on," Josie argued.

"That makes no difference," Mrs Daley replied. "As I recall, the last time I saw Heather we had some difficulty carrying on a conversation. I suppose there's a generation gap. It will be a lot more pleasant for her if there's someone else her own age here."

Not when that someone else is me, Josie thought. She hoped her face hadn't revealed her reaction, but Mrs Daley was peering at her keenly. For someone whose eyesight wasn't too great, she certainly had no problem reading expressions.

"Don't you like my granddaughter?" she asked bluntly.

Josie hesitated. She thought about all the nasty stunts Heather had pulled on Cat. Of course, in all fairness, Cat had managed a few schemes of her own, too. But she remembered how Heather had tried to arrange for Becka to get hit in the face with a pie in front of the whole school. And how she'd made Todd lie to Coach Meadows, telling him that none of the boys wanted Josie on the basketball team. How could she say anything about Heather without letting on that, in her opinion, the girl was practically evil?

It was best to say nothing at all. "I guess I just don't know her very well."

"Well, here's a chance for you to get to know her," Mrs Daley stated.

Josie's insides were queasy, but she managed a bright smile. "That's right. Now, what can I do to help you get ready?"

"Is there anything you can do with my hair?" the woman asked hopefully, patting her unruly grey mop.

"I'm no hairdresser," Josie replied, "but I'll give it a shot."

By the time she'd tamed Mrs Daley's hair with a brush and a few bobby pins, Sue was back from the bakery. Josie helped arrange the pastries and the cake on plates and set water to boil for tea. Then Sue took off on more errands, and Josie settled down with Mrs Daley to wait for Heather. She was about to suggest a card game when the doorbell rang.

"I'll get it," Josie said. She stretched her lips into a grin and went to the door.

"Hi, Heather." She forced some warmth into her words.

Heather's smile was even more artificial than

her own. "Hello, Josie. So nice to see you. Grandmother, dear! It's been ages!"

Whose fault is that? Josie asked silently as Heather brushed her lips against her grand-mother's cheek. "I'll get the tea," Josie announced, leaving Heather and Mrs Daley together on the sofa.

She took her time in the kitchen. Despite what Mrs Daley had said, Josie felt sure they'd need some time alone, to talk about private family stuff. But when she returned with the teapot, the living room was silent.

"Tell me about your classes," Mrs Daley said to Heather. "Do you have good teachers? Are you enjoying school?"

"I told you, grandmother, everything's fine." Heather seemed more interested in watching Josie pour tea. "How long have you been working here?"

"This is my second week. If you can call it working. It's more like fun for me." She handed a cup of tea to Heather.

Heather took a sip, eyeing Josie thoughtfully over the rim of her cup. "How did you find out about this job?"

"I read about it in the *Green Falls Daily News*. It's weird. I was complaining about having to read newspapers for school. But if it wasn't for that assignment, I probably never would have found out about this job."

"Is that where you saw the ad for the horse, too?" Mrs Daley asked.

"What horse?" Heather asked.

There was something about the way her expression became suddenly alert that made Josie uneasy.

"Oh, just a horse I'm saving up to buy. His name is Sunshine. He's a ten-year-old quarter horse."

"That's nice," Heather said.

The room fell silent. "Do you like horses, dear?" Mrs Daley asked Heather.

"Not particularly." Heather turned back to Josie. "Aren't horses very expensive?"

Josie nodded. "It's going to take me a while to save all the money I need."

"I do wish you'd let me lend you the rest of the money," Mrs Daley said.

Heather rose. "I have to go now."

Mrs Daley's face fell. "So soon? Heather, you just got here!"

"I've got shopping to do, Grandmother. There's a big dance coming up at school. I had the most perfect dress all picked out. But when I went to Danielle's Boutique to buy it, someone else had put it aside! Isn't that awful?"

Josie wondered why Heather was directing that remark at *her*. "Awful," she murmured.

Mrs Daley pointed to the untouched plates. "But you haven't eaten anything!"

"I'll be back again soon," Heather said. She threw a quick kiss in her grandmother's direction. "Bye, Josie."

Mrs Daley struggled to get to her feet, but Heather was out the door before she could stand up. Josie watched as the woman sank back heavily into her seat and gazed wistfully at the closed door. She had a strong urge to wrap her arms around Mrs Daley, but her natural reserve held her back.

Then Mrs Daley turned back to Josie and smiled a little sadly. "How would you like to adopt a grandmother?"

That was all it took for Josie to drop her reserve.

Becka sat behind the counter at Morgan's Country Foods with her elbows on the countertop and her chin resting in her hands. A man stood over by the fruit bins, picking out apples. A woman strolled down an aisle, pausing to examine the selection of jams. That was it – two customers. Becka had expected customers to be beating down the door by now.

"Why so glum?" Ben asked.

"I don't understand," Becka said. "I thought my ad was going to help business."

"Don't worry about it," Ben said. "You did what you could."

Annie stroked Becka's hair. "Every business goes through slumps, honey. We'll come out of this one sooner or later."

"But it was such a good ad," Becka insisted. "I can't figure out why it didn't work."

"Maybe people didn't see it," Annie suggested. "Actually, I don't think we ever saw it. Did we, Ben?"

"No, but I'm sure it was a persuasive masterpiece."

"I thought so, too, but I guess I was wrong." Becka fumbled in her knapsack for a copy of the *Green Gazette*. She opened it to the ad page and handed the paper to Annie. Ben read it aloud over his wife's shoulder.

"A message from Morgan's Country Foods. Do you want to lose weight? Are you losing your hair? Is your face breaking out? Then try our all-natural miracle foods and watch your problems disappear."

Listening to the words, Becka closed her eyes and once again marvelled at how convincing the ad sounded. Surely there were fat people and bald people and people with bad complexions in Green Falls. Why weren't they here?

Suddenly, she realized that Ben and Annie were oddly silent. She opened her eyes. Her parents' expressions were startling. Instead of the beaming, proud faces she expected to see, both of them looked completely aghast.

"Becka!" Annie gasped. "How could you write something like this?"

Becka fumbled with her words. "Because . . . because I figured people would buy anything that could help them lose weight or grow hair."

Ben gazed at her in horror. "But nothing we sell in this store does that!"

Did they think she was stupid or something? "I know that," Becka replied. She looked at them in confusion. What were they getting so upset about?

"Then why did you write this?" Ben asked. His voice was getting louder.

"To get people to buy the stuff we *do* sell. To make it all sound special."

"But Becka, what you've written here – this isn't true!" Annie exclaimed.

"It doesn't have to be completely true," Becka said. "It's an ad." She noted with alarm that Ben's face was getting red. "Ads lie all the time. I bought some stuff that was supposed to get rid of my birthmark and it didn't work."

Now Ben's face was taking on a purple hue. "That doesn't mean you have the right to lie. Becka, this is false advertising! Do you know what kind of reputation we could get if we make false claims about our goods?"

Becka shrunk back.

"Ben, calm down," Annie said. "She didn't know any better. Honey, we realise you just wanted to help. But something like this can do more harm than good. Like that stuff you bought for your birthmark. Since it doesn't do what it said it would do, you wouldn't buy it again, would you? Or recommend it to your friends?"

"I guess not," Becka admitted.

"And it's not just bad business," Annie continued. "It's morally wrong to lie like this."

Slowly, Becka nodded. What Annie said made sense. But there was still something Becka didn't understand. "How do all those ads get away with lying? I saw an ad for shampoo once that said it would make my hair look shinier. I tried it, and it didn't make my hair shinier at all."

Ben's face was beginning to return to its normal colour. "Some ads do lie. Or at least, exaggerate and stretch the truth. But that doesn't make it right. That's one of the reasons I got out of the advertising business. I'd write ads and then I'd feel ashamed, because I knew I wasn't being totally honest about a product."

Becka hung her head. "I'm sorry."

Ben tousled her hair. "At least you've learned something from this."

"Can we just forget I ever wrote this?" Becka asked.

Ben shook his head. "No, honey, I'm afraid you'll have to make up for it. You have to write a retraction."

"A what?"

"A retraction. Another ad saying that the statements made in this ad were not true, and that there's nothing sold at Morgan's Country Foods that will help a person lose weight or grow hair or . . . what was the other one?"

Becka felt silly even saying it. "Clear up a bad complexion."

"You have to apologise for printing misleading claims. And the ad should be printed in the next copy of your newspaper."

Becka thought of how Jason and the rest of the staff would react to that. "Everyone's going to think I'm pretty goofy."

"Maybe," Ben said. "But it's better for people to think you're goofy than to think you have no ethics. Right?"

Becka sighed. "Okay." She slid off her stool. "I'll go write it now."

"And put the Closed sign on the door, please," Annie called to her. Becka did and walked out. As she headed across the road, a car pulled up and a man she'd never seen before got out. He started towards the store.

"We're closed," Becka called to him.

"Oh, too bad," he said. He looked disappointed.

"Was there something special you wanted?" Becka asked. She was thinking she could run back in and get it for him, if it was really important.

"I came about this," he said, holding up a newspaper. It was the *Green Gazette,* and as Becka drew closer, she saw that it was opened to the page with her ad.

At least one person had been attracted by it. But that didn't lift her spirits. "I guess I'd better tell you, none of that is true."

The man's eyebrows went up. "You mean, there's nothing sold here that aids weight loss or hair growth?"

"No. Nothing at all." Becka wondered why he was so interested. He looked pretty thin to her. But maybe his hair was thinning on top, where she couldn't see it.

"How do you know this?"

"Because I'm Becka Morgan. My parents own this store. And I wrote the ad."

"I see." The man studied her. "Did your parents approve of this ad?"

Becka shook her head fervently. "They're making me write a retraction."

"I see," he said again. "Why did you make these claims in the first place?"

Becka hesitated. It wasn't really any of his business. But there was something about his friendly eyes, his interest, that made her feel like talking. "Because business hasn't been so good lately. We haven't been getting a lot of customers. And I thought it would be okay to lie a little – okay, a lot – if it would get people to come in. But my parents said it was wrong. That's why I have to write a retraction."

The man smiled. "Well, good luck with it, Becka." He started back towards the car.

"Come again," Becka called after him. "Everything we sell is really good. And all natural. And not too expensive."

The man smiled and waved. Strangely enough, she felt better, maybe because the man hadn't laughed at her. Confessing out loud hadn't been so hard. Now she had to put it on paper, and hope her classmates wouldn't laugh either.

Seven

Cat wore an unusually cheerful smile when she entered the dining room at breakfast the next morning. "What are you so happy about?" Becka asked.

"It's Thursday," Cat replied.

Annie handed her a glass of orange juice. "What's special about Thursdays?"

"No work."

Ben put the newspaper down and raised his eyebrows. "Isn't the job going well?"

"Oh, no, it's fine," Cat said quickly. "It's just that, well, sometimes it's nice not to work. Becka, would you pass the toast, please?"

Becka shoved the plate of toast in Cat's general direction. As Cat buttered a slice, she added, "I really like counting my money."

"How much have you saved?" Josie asked.

"Twenty dollars. How about you?" She didn't care for the smug expression that crossed Josie's face.

"Seventy dollars."

"Seventy!"

Ben winced. "Cat, sweetie, don't scream so early in the morning."

In a slightly less loud shriek, Cat asked, "How did you save seventy dollars already?"

Josie bit into her toast, chewed, and swallowed before answering. "I work more hours than you, I started my job before you, and I guess I make more money."

Cat frowned as she considered this. "How long do you have to work before asking for a raise?"

"Longer than a week is usually advised," Annie replied dryly. "Cat, I wouldn't hit Sally and George up for a raise just now. They've only had the inn open for a week, and they're probably struggling."

"Getting a business on its feet takes time," Ben added. "As we all know."

"Maybe they should advertise," Josie said with a mischievous glance in Becka's direction.

"Yeah," Cat chimed in. "Stay at the Green Falls Inn and – and grow six inches."

"Girls, don't tease," Annie remonstrated.

"Very funny," Becka muttered.

Cat returned to the original subject. "If I had seventy dollars, I could get my dress off credit right now."

"Credit," Josie repeated. She snapped her fingers. "That's why Heather gave me the evil eye yesterday. She said she'd wanted to buy a dress at Danielle's Boutique, but someone had already taken it. And she gave me the meanest look. Cat, did Heather want the same dress as you?"

Cat nodded. "I guess she found out that I was the one who put it on one side. I'll bet she's mad!"

Annie looked at her curiously. "Why does that make you so happy?"

Cat scrambled in her mind for a reasonable explanation. Somehow, for months she'd managed to keep her ongoing war with Heather Beaumont a secret from her parents. Instinct told her they wouldn't exactly approve. "Well, Heather's not the nicest girl in the world. And it's fun knowing I've got something she wants."

Ben shook his head reprovingly. "That's not a very good attitude, Cat. What are you going to do next, steal her boyfriend?"

Cat practically choked on her juice. "Uh, could you guys hurry up? I want to get to school early. I have to do something before homeroom."

"I'm ready if you are," Annie said.

On the way to school, a light snow began to fall. "Look at those greasers," Becka said as they got out of the car. "Sitting on the steps in the snow."

She and Josie hurried towards the entrance.

Cat lagged behind. As soon as her sisters disappeared into the building, Cat casually edged towards one of the guys on the steps.

"Think we're going to get a real snowfall?" she asked.

Sid Belcher sneered at her. "What do I look like, a weatherman?"

Cat pretended he'd just said something funny. She tossed her head, laughed brightly, and gave him a sidelong look. It was a move she'd used a zillion times, and it never failed to have an impact.

Until now. "What's so funny?" Sid growled.

"What do you think?" Cat asked in a teasing voice.

"How should I know? You're the one who's laughing."

Cat tried to recall if they'd ever actually met before. "I'm Cat Morgan."

"Your name's Cat?" His lips parted, revealing yellowish teeth. "You got claws?" He started laughing at his own unamusing joke. It was an ugly laugh that matched his face.

Cat gave up and went on into the school. She'd always thought she'd do anything to upset Heather Beaumont. But there were limits.

Josie was beat. Basketball practice had gone on much longer than usual. Coach Meadows was trying to make up for cutting back on the practice sessions. Now it was almost six o'clock, which meant she wouldn't be able to go see Sunshine and be home in time for dinner. The snow had stopped, but there was plenty of wet slush to walk through. She'd left her wool scarf back in the locker room, but she didn't have the energy to go back and get it. She was cold, hungry, and totally exhausted.

She cheered up by reminding herself that it wouldn't be too much longer before Sunshine would be there at home, waiting for her. And her mood improved considerably when she walked into the house.

Ben was at the fireplace, stoking a blazing fire which cast a warm glow over the living room. Becka was curled in the rocking chair, a book in her lap. In the dining room, Cat was setting the table for dinner. Good smells floated out from the kitchen, where Josie could hear Annie singing.

"Boy, is it good to be home," Josie sighed, slipping out of her coat.

"Honey, you should have called me," Ben said. "I would have picked you up."

"Oh, that's okay. Something smells great," Josie said.

Annie came out from the kitchen. "Chilli and cornbread. Josie, take those wet shoes off right this minute. I don't want you catching cold."

Josie happily obliged. She used to think she'd

hate having people fuss over her. But every now and then it was very pleasant.

The phone rang in the kitchen. "I'll get it," Annie said.

"I turned in my retraction to the *Green Gazette*," Becka announced.

"Did the editor give you any grief about it?" Josie asked.

"Not really. In fact, Jason told me this was the first time the *Gazette* ever printed a retraction. He said it made him feel like it was a real newspaper." She made a little face. "I still feel pretty stupid about it."

"Look at it this way," Josie said cheerfully. "It's more publicity for the store."

Annie called from the dining room. "Josie, Ben, would you come back here for a minute?"

"Sure," Josie said. "Did you burn the cornbread?" Annie had yet to completely master the mysteries of cooking. But one look at Annie's face told her that whatever it was, it had nothing to do with food. Cat's curious eyes followed Josie as she went through the dining room to the kitchen.

"What's the matter?" Ben asked once the three of them were together.

Annie's face was troubled. "That was a Mr Beaumont on the phone."

"Heather's father?" Josie asked, puzzled. "Why would he be calling here?"

Annie spoke in a soft voice. "He's also Mrs Daley's son-in-law."

A sudden fear gripped Josie. "Oh no! Has something happened to Mrs Daley?"

"No, dear, she's fine," Annie said hastily. "But . . ." She seemed to be having a hard time saying something. Josie waited anxiously.

Annie bit her lip. "Mr Beaumont doesn't want you to work for Mrs Daley any more."

Josie heard the words, but they didn't sink in right away.

"Why not?" Ben asked.

"He wouldn't say. All he told me, and I quote, was that 'Josie's services are no longer required.' "

Now that Josie had absorbed the message, she immediately reached for the telephone.

"I'm going to call Mrs Daley and find out what this is all about."

Annie put a gentle restraining hand on Josie's arm. "He also said you weren't to call her or see her."

Josie gasped. "But that's crazy! Mrs Daley likes me! She wouldn't want me fired!"

"Darling, I know you feel awful about this," Annie said. "But Mr Beaumont is a member of her family, and we have to respect his wishes."

"But this doesn't make sense!" Josie cried. She simply couldn't believe she wasn't going to see Mrs Daley again. Then something else hit her, and she clapped a hand to her mouth. "Sunshine . . ." she breathed.

"What?" Ben asked.

Josie clenched her fists. There was no point in keeping it a secret anymore. "Sunshine. He's a horse that's for sale. I've been saving my money to buy him. That's why I got the job in the first place."

"Why didn't you tell us about this?" Annie asked.

"Well, you were worried about the store, and I didn't want you to think I was asking for something you couldn't afford. I was going to wait till I had all the money saved and then ask if I could buy him." She felt something wet on her cheek. Furiously, she brushed the tear away.

Annie and Ben exchanged agonised looks. "How much does the horse cost?" Ben asked.

"Four hundred dollars. I've saved seventy."

Ben thought for a moment. "Maybe if I talked to the owner, he'd accept a down payment on the horse."

"You mean, put him on credit?" Josie asked hopefully. "Like Cat's dress?"

Ben nodded. "Where's the phone book?"

Josie told him the owner's name, and Ben looked him up in the directory. Then he dialled.

"Hello, this is Ben Morgan. I'm the father of Josie, the girl who's interested in buying your

horse, Sunshine. I wanted to ask if – what?"
There was a pause. "I see. Thank you." He
hung up.

"What did he say?" Annie asked.

Ben looked like *he* wanted to cry. "Josie . . ."

Somehow, Josie already knew what he was
going to say. "He sold Sunshine."

Ben nodded. Silently, with their eyes filled
with love and sympathy, he and Annie gazed at
Josie. But this was a moment when Josie didn't
want any fussing.

"I . . . I think I'll go to my room for a while."

As she passed through the dining room, she
was aware of Cat and Becka watching her.
"What's wrong?" Cat asked.

Josie was suprised to hear her own voice
coming out clear and steady. "I've lost my job.
And Sunshine's been sold." Only at the end
did her voice crack. She ran up the stairs so
she could cry in private.

Standing in the centre of a bedroom at the
inn, Cat wondered if losing a job was really
such a tragedy. Okay, maybe for Josie it was.
She remembered how upset Josie had been the
night before, how she couldn't even eat dinner.
She had looked the same this morning and had
barely touched her breakfast.

Well, it was different for Josie. She'd actually
liked working. But as Cat struggled to get a

fitted sheet corner off a bed, she thought she wouldn't mind losing this job. And as soon as she had enough money for her dress, she would.

Thinking of the dress made her think of the Turnaround dance, which made her think about a date. She recalled her encounter the day before with Sid Belcher and shuddered. For the millionth time, she wondered why Heather wanted to go out with him. Maybe she was into bad guys. Cat knew there were girls who screamed over those guys in heavy metal bands, with their tough attitudes and tattoos and stringy hair. Not Cat. Even the tantalizing temptation of spiting Heather wasn't enough to drive her in that direction.

No, she wasn't about to go after the date Heather wanted. But at least she'd have the dress.

The sheet corner wouldn't come up so Cat gave it a hard tug. Then she groaned as the sheet ripped.

Naturally, Miss Andrews would choose that minute to check on her work. The housekeeper gazed at the torn sheet in despair. "You are undoubtedly the worst excuse for a maid I've ever seen," she announced. "Morgan, you are positively incompetent. Utterly worthless."

By now, Cat was so accustomed to Miss

Andrews' criticisms and rebukes that they went in one ear and out the other. She didn't even bother to apologise, which seemed to make Miss Andrews even angrier.

"The only reason you're kept on here is because your parents are friends of the Laytons."

"I know that," Cat said airily. "It doesn't bother me in the least." Cat sensed she was being rude, but she was beyond caring.

Miss Andrews pressed her lips together so hard they turned white. Cat tried to find her manners.

"What would you like me to do now, Miss Andrews?" she asked politely.

"We can't afford for you to ruin any more sheets," the housekeeper replied through her clenched lips. "Go downstairs and dust."

Cat scurried out of the room. As she went down the hall, a door opened. "Hi, Cat."

Bailey was grinning. Remembering how he'd witnessed her escapade on Monday, Cat flushed and ducked her head. "Hello," she murmured and kept on walking towards the stairs. He followed her.

"Do you go to the same school as Heather?"

Cat nodded.

"I'll be starting there next week."

"That's nice." Cat eyed him warily. He hadn't exposed her secret to Heather. Would he remain as silent at school?

"I hear it's an okay place," he remarked. "I mean, considering that it's a school."

He was trying to be funny. Automatically, without even thinking, Cat went into her act: head toss, bright laugh, sidelong look. Then she felt stupid. How much impact could that have when she was dressed as a maid?

But, to her amazement, she recognised the expression on Bailey's face. She'd seen that same expression on Todd's face, and on the faces of other boys she'd flirted with (not counting Sid Belcher). She caught her breath. Was there a chance, a remote possibility, that he liked her? Even wearing an *apron?* Or was he just leading her on?

There was no time to find out, because his mother stepped out of her room. "Come on, Bailey, we have to get over to the Beaumonts'."

Cat allowed them to pass ahead of her and start down the stairs. But she was pleased when Bailey turned his head and smiled back at her.

For the next hour, Cat listlessly passed her rag over the various pieces of furniture in the dining room, barely moving any bits of dust around. Bailey's cute face was firmly implanted in her brain, and despite her efforts, she couldn't push him out.

He'd be the centre of female attention next week at Green Falls Junior High. There was no doubt about it. Girls would flock to him. There would be Cat, sauntering down the hall in her green sweater, hair loose and flowing, perfectly groomed. Maybe Bailey would forget that he'd first seen her as a maid. . . .

"Aren't you finished in here yet?" Miss Andrews' sharp voice ended her reverie. She ran a finger along a sideboard, then looked at the finger in disgust.

"I'm going into the lobby now," Cat replied quickly, and hurried out.

She returned to her fantasies as she lightly stroked the mantle over the fireplace with her rag. A thought struck her. No, it was too outrageous to contemplate. But then, this was just a daydream, so she might as well indulge herself.

What if . . . what if she asked Bailey to the Turnaround? Suddenly, she could see herself, walking into the decorated gym, arm in arm with him. Everyone's eyes would be on them. What a couple they'd make! Cat in her black velvet, Bailey in a black suit – no, a light-coloured one, to set off his gorgeous tan. She had a clear vision of Heather, with that grungy Sid Belcher, eyeing them in envy as they floated onto the dance floor. Oh, it would be awesome. . . .

The image exploded with a crash. Cat jumped back. Fragments of a big vase that had stood on the mantle just seconds before lay all over the floor.

Miss Andrews came running out of the dining room. Sally Layton flew out from the office behind the reception desk. They both stood there, speechless.

Cat gulped. "Uh, I'm sorry. I guess I wasn't looking where I dusted."

"My vase from China," Sally moaned. She went over to where it had fallen and knelt down.

"Can it be fixed?" Cat asked.

Sally shook her head. "It's beyond repair."

Cat felt awful. "I'm *really* sorry. I'll . . . I'll pay for it." She hated asking the next question, but she had to. "Was it very expensive?"

"I'm afraid so," Sally said, picking up the pieces.

Miss Andrews spoke stiffly. "Mrs Layton, this girl is a walking disaster. She can't dust, she can't sweep, she can't even take sheets off a bed. I've told you this before. I realise that she's the daughter of your friends, but it's my duty to tell you that she has no business working as a maid."

Sally rose from the floor. "I'm sure Cat didn't intend to break the vase," she murmured tentatively, but the housekeeper didn't let her continue. She folded her arms across her chest and faced Sally with a look of determination.

"Either that girl goes or I go."

The look of horror that crossed Sally's face

108

told Cat she didn't want to lose her house-keeper.

"Oh, Miss Andrews . . ." Sally began, but her voice trailed off as the housekeeper remained steadfast. Sally sighed heavily and turned to Cat.

"Cat, dear, I'm sorry, but it looks like things aren't working out."

Cat froze as she absorbed the implication of the words. "But I've got a dress on credit! I'll be more careful, I promise!"

Her plea seemed to have an effect on Sally, and the woman once again turned to Miss Andrews. The housekeeper shook her head firmly.

"I'm sorry, Cat," Sally repeated. She really did look regretful.

There was nothing left to say. Feeling like her world was crumbling, Cat made her way to the little powder room. In a daze, she removed her uniform and put on her skirt and blouse. She gathered up her schoolbooks and purse and went out.

"I'm truly sorry, Cat," Sally Layton called to her again as Cat dragged herself back through the lobby towards the door. But all the apologies in the world weren't going to pay for that dress.

Cat hadn't bothered to button up her coat, but she didn't even feel the cold as she stepped outside. She was positively numb with shock.

Then she saw a car pulling up. Bailey and his mother got out. Mrs Hudson hurried to the inn, but Bailey stopped when he saw Cat.

"Leaving already?" he asked.

Cat nodded, but she didn't explain. It was bad enough for him to know she had been a maid. How could she admit she'd been a failure as one?

She turned away from him and started walking.

"Wait!" Bailey called.

She paused and let him catch up to her. "I was just talking to Heather," he said. "She was telling me about this dance, this Turnaround thing."

The impact of his words hit her like a rock. No, more like a gallon of water poured on her head when she was already drowning.

"Are you going?" he asked.

Cat couldn't be sure if the word actually left her mouth, or if her lips had just formed it. "No." She whirled around and flew off.

So Heather was taking Bailey Hudson to the Turnaround dance. Everything became very clear. Heather never intended to ask Sid Belcher. It was a setup. She'd planted hints, knowing Britt was in the bathroom when she was talking about him, and again with Josie. Her mean, nasty little mind had assumed that Cat would ask any boy she thought Heather wanted to ask.

And now she'd get the black velvet dress, too. Cat was too upset to do any arithmetic calculations, but she knew that whatever amount of money was needed to pay off the dress, she'd never have it in time.

Heather would be going to the Turnaround with the cutest boy and the prettiest dress. As for Cat, all she knew was that in the entire universe at this moment, there couldn't be anyone more miserable than she was.

Eight

It was like a grey cloud had fallen on the Morgan household, Cat decided the next morning. There wasn't a cheerful face at the breakfast table. Outside, the world sparkled from the sun's rays on the new-fallen snow, and inside the delicious smell of cinnamon rose from the steaming bowls of oatmeal, but neither of those things had any effect on the general atmosphere.

Josie, with her elbows on the table, stirred her oatmeal without lifting a spoonful to her mouth. She was still pale and puffy eyed. Cat wondered if she herself looked as bad. She was certainly entitled to, every bit as much as Josie was.

Becka was eating, but her forehead was puckered, which meant she was worrying. Every few minutes, she let out a soft sigh. Cat couldn't see her expression, but she knew she was totally incapable of making even the slightest attempt at a smile or conversation.

"We're certainly a jolly bunch today," Ben commented. It was his third remark of that type. No one responded. Ben shook his head in resignation and returned to his breakfast.

Annie took a stab at it. In an overly bright voice, she asked, "Do you girls have any special plans for today?"

Three heads moved from side to side.

"Ben and I are doing inventory at the store today," she went on. "We thought we'd take advantage of the quiet. If you don't have anything else to do, you can come and help out if you'd like. We'll turn it into a party!"

This suggestion received three unenthusiastic nods.

Annie sighed heavily. "Girls, I know everything seems bleak right now, but things will get better, I promise. Josie, there will be other horses for sale. Cat, you'll find another dress, one that's more within your means. And Becka . . . Becka, I'm not sure I even know *why* you're depressed.

"My retraction's coming out in the *Green Gazette* on Monday," Becka told her. "I'm afraid everyone at school is going to make fun of me."

It was hard for Cat to drum up any sympathy. Becka's concern was nothing compared to *her* problems.

"If people tease you, just laugh along with them," Annie advised.

Becka managed a wan smile, but it was clear what she thought of that idea.

"Ben," Annie said. "Help!"

"What?" Ben asked.

"Look at your daughters! Have you ever seen three more miserable faces?"

Ben made another futile attempt at humour. "They're teenagers. They're supposed to be depressed, right?"

Annie raised her hands in an I-give-up gesture. The phone rang and she leaped off the chair as if she were escaping. Becka let out another of her soft sighs, and Cat turned to her in irritation.

"Quit moaning," she demanded.

Becka became indignant. "Look who's talking. You've been whining non-stop since yesterday."

"I've got a right to," Cat retorted. "I've got *real* problems."

"Some problems," Josie growled. "You can't buy a dumb dress. That's really serious."

"Just as serious as a stupid horse," Cat shot back. "And all Becka's carrying on about is a silly newspaper that no one even reads."

"Oh, yeah? My problems are just as real as yours!" Becka argued.

"All of you, stop it," Ben ordered. "You've got problems. Your mother and I have problems. We're all going to be sympathetic to each other and stop feeling sorry for ourselves. Case closed."

That stilled the argument for the time being, but the girls were still shooting hostile looks at one another. Annie returned from the kitchen.

"That was Sally Layton, from the inn. Cat, she'd like you to come by today so that she can give you your pay from yesterday."

"Goody, goody," Cat murmured. "Eight dollars." She got a glimpse of Annie's rebuking face and rose hastily. "I'll go get ready."

Josie got up, too. "I'll do the dishes."

"I'll help you," Becka offered.

"Thanks," Josie said, "but I'd rather be alone." Cat rolled her eyes. Josie sounded *so* tragic.

"You can come to the store with Ben and me, Becka," Annie said.

Cat went up to her room and sat down at the dressing table mirror. Studying her reflection, she decided she didn't look as bad as Josie, but pretty bad, nonetheless. She couldn't go to the inn looking like a pathetic, downtrodden nobody. There was a chance she could run into Bailey. She might as well show him who he *could* have been escorting to the Turnaround.

When Cat finished a careful application of make-up, she put on her newest jeans, a green sweater that made her eyes look like emeralds, and boots. Then she gave herself a satisfied once-over in the mirror. She looked cool, confident, and totally together – the opposite of how she felt.

115

Beyond her reflection, she saw Josie standing at her door. "Are you going to the store?"

"Yeah, I guess so," Cat said, inserting small gold hoops into her pierced ears. "When I get back from the inn."

"Tell Ben and Annie I'll be there in a little while. I've got something to do first."

Cat noticed that Josie had her parka on. "Where are you going?"

"To see Mrs Daley."

Shocked, Cat tore her eyes from the mirror. "Josie! You can't do that! Mr Beaumont told Annie you're not supposed to see her!"

"I don't care," Josie said. "Look, there's nothing I can do about Sunshine. But I've got to find out why Mrs Daley doesn't want me around anymore."

"You're going to get into trouble," Cat warned. But Josie had her jaw set in that obstinate way that told Cat nothing would change her mind. She stuffed her hands in her pockets and took off.

Cat couldn't help admiring her determination and guts. Of course, she thought that Josie should use them for more important purposes, but still, Cat respected her bravery.

Cat opened her jewellery box and took out the twenty dollars she'd saved from her job. Maybe if she still felt really down after leaving the inn, she'd go buy herself something. That was always a surefire cure for the blues. She went downstairs, got her coat, and left.

Now that she wasn't working there anymore, the inn had stopped looking like a prison. With the clean white snow nestled on its roof and window ledges, it was charming again.

Inside, she glanced around furtively for Miss Andrews and breathed a sigh of relief that the housekeeper was nowhere in sight. Sally Layton was behind the reception desk.

"Hello, Cat, I'm glad you came by. I hope there are no hard feelings."

Cat didn't want to give her the satisfaction of a real response, but the woman sounded so sincere that she relented and forced a small smile.

Sally handed her an envelope. "There's your salary for yesterday. And a little something extra as, well, a show of appreciation."

Cat accepted it with a gracious nod. "Thank you."

"Excuse me, dear. I have to see about something in the dining room." As soon as Sally disappeared, Cat tore open the envelope. As she expected, there were eight dollar bills. And a long, pale blue slip of paper. She pulled the paper out, then drew in her breath sharply.

It was a gift certificate to Danielle's Boutique in the amount of thirty-five dollars! Suddenly, her head was spinning. Was this for real?

Cat snatched a pencil from the desk and a copy of the inn's brochure. On the back of the brochure she scrawled $67.50. That was what she owed on the dress. Then she put down the total amount she'd made working: $28. She added that to $35. It came to $63. She subtracted that from $67.50. Four dollars and fifty cents. Exactly what she had left from this week's allowance.

In amazement, she did the sums over again. It came out the same. There was no doubt in Cat's mind that she was witnessing a miracle. Her heart was beating with excitement. The dress was hers!

Just as she was stuffing the envelope into her purse, she heard a voice say, "Hello, Cat."

Cat looked up. "Hello, Bailey," she said coolly. He was looking slightly less than sure of himself.

"How come you ran off like that yesterday?" he asked.

"I was in a hurry," she said. "Now, let's see . . . oh yes, you were telling me about your date with Heather." Cat assumed a bored expression.

"What date with Heather?"

"For the Turnaround dance."

Bailey scratched his head. "I don't have a date with Heather for the Turnaround dance."

For once in her life, Cat was at a loss for

words. "But, what about . . . I mean, you said—"

"I just said she told me about the dance." He gave her an abashed grin. "Okay, just between us, she *did* ask me. But I didn't say yes."

Cat stared at him blankly. "Why not?"

Bailey suddenly became very interested in his shoes. "Well, because . . . I was hoping *you'd* ask me."

"Becka, would you see if that woman needs any help?" Annie asked hurriedly. She was trying to ring up a sale on the cash register for one customer and point out where the wholewheat flour was to another. Over by the bins of fresh fruit, Ben had a line of people waiting for him to weigh their bags.

Becka sailed off towards the woman who was wandering down an aisle. "Can I help you?"

"I was trying to find your maple syrup."

"I'm afraid we're sold out," Becka replied. But we'll be getting more on Monday. Have you tried our jams?"

The woman brightened. "No, but I'd like to."

Becka led her to the rapidly diminishing selection of jams. Leaving the woman to contemplate the flavours, she hurried away to help another couple who had just walked in.

It had been like that since the store opened.

Of course, they usually did get a few more customers on Saturdays than any other day. But never like this. There hadn't been a moment all morning when there were fewer than a dozen people in Morgan's Country Foods.

They could forget about doing an inventory. There was hardly anything left on the shelves to count and not a minute available to count what *was* there. Becka hadn't stopped moving since they opened the doors, and her ears were ringing from the constant jingles of the cash register and the bell over the door.

Ben and Annie looked just as bewildered as she did. But none of them had had a free moment to talk about it.

Back at the counter, a woman had one bag in her arms and was trying to lift another. "Can I carry one of those to your car for you?" Becka asked.

"No, thank you, dear," the woman said as she got a firm grip on her bags. Then she beamed at her. "Are you the little girl in the story?"

Becka was so startled by the question that she wasn't even insulted at being called a little girl. "What story?"

Annie, too, was looking at the woman in bewilderment. "Becka was in a story?"

"In the newspaper!" the woman said. "You mean, you haven't seen it?"

Becka had a feeling the woman wasn't talking about the *Green Gazette*. Sure enough, the woman set down her bags, fumbled in her purse, and pulled out a clipping. "It's from this morning's edition of the *Daily News*. Here, read it. In fact, why don't you keep it? It's not often that a person gets her name in the paper!" She hoisted up her bags and left.

Annie and Becka put their heads together and read the clipping. It was a regular feature from the newspaper, a column called "This and That," which reported funny little goings-on in Green Falls. At the top was a photo of the man who wrote it. He looked familiar. Becka drew in her breath. "That's the man I talked to on Wednesday when I was leaving the store! I told him we were closed."

"He came back on Thursday," Annie murmured as she read the column.

The first paragraph was about a Girl Scout who had sold more cookies than anyone in the state. The second paragraph was about a family's successful search for a lost dog.

The third paragraph made Becka and Annie gasp in unison.

In an attempt to bolster business at her family's store, Morgan's Country Foods, Becka Morgan, a student at Green Falls Junior High, placed an ad in her school

121

newspaper in which she proclaimed the magical curative powers of the products available in the store. Curious as to these remarkable claims, this reporter visited the store in question, and while he was unable to locate any item which might stem the loss of his hair, he found the sweetest maple syrup, the juiciest jams, the tastiest breads, and the freshest produce available in these parts. Definitely worth a visit! By the way, Becka's parents were not pleased with their daughter's well-intentioned but misleading claims, and Becka has been ordered to write a retraction. It's nice to know our merchants are committed to truth in advertising!

As Becka and Annie looked at each other in astonishment, a man plunked some purchases on the counter. He saw what they were reading and nodded. "You know, I didn't even know this place was here until I read that this morning!"

Another customer fell in line behind him. "Yes, wasn't that cute? And I must say, everything here does look delicious. You'll be seeing a lot of me!"

"That's nice," Annie said, her eyes glassy. "Ben!"

When he joined them, she handed him the

clipping. Still looking dazed, Annie started ringing up the purchases.

"Good grief!" Ben blurted out. "What – how—?"

"Excuse me," Becka said sweetly. "But we've got customers to help." And she sailed off on cloud nine.

Nine

Josie strode along rapidly until she reached the cottage. Then she hesitated. What if Mrs Daley refused to see her? Could she bear having someone she'd thought was a friend slam a door in her face?

She had to risk it. It would be better to know than to always wonder what she had done wrong. She marched up the pathway to the door and rapped firmly.

Sue Campbell opened the door. "Josie!" It was evident she was surprised to see her. Josie waited for Sue's quick smile but it didn't come.

"I'm here to see Mrs Daley."

From the back of the house, a voice rung out. "Who is it, Sue?"

"It's Josie Morgan," Sue called back.

"Well, let her in!"

Sue stepped aside, allowing Josie room to pass. But as she did, she whispered, "Don't upset her, Josie."

Josie was bewildered. "Upset Mrs Daley? Why would I do that?"

Mrs Daley didn't seem at all upset to see her.

She wore a big smile as she hobbled towards Josie. "What a nice surprise! I wondered if I'd ever see you again. Sit down, dear."

Now Josie was really confused. Mrs Daley wasn't faking her pleasure. Then why had Josie been forbidden to visit?

She waited for Mrs Daley to ease herself onto the sofa and then sat alongside her. "It's good to see you, too. How have you been?"

Mrs Daley gazed at her steadily. "I must say, I was rather disappointed in you, young lady. And a little hurt when my son-in-law told me you had resigned."

Josie sat up straight. "Resigned?"

"My daughter's been taking your place," Mrs Daley continued. "Actually, it's been good for both of us. I feel Gloria and I have drifted apart, and this time together is bringing us closer."

Sue peered out the window. "Here comes your daughter now. Oh Mr Beaumont's with her, too. I'll be off now."

Mrs Daley hoisted herself up and went to the door. A wave of panic swept through Josie. "Mr Beaumont?" She couldn't imagine what his reaction would be at finding her there. She looked around the room frantically. Maybe she should hide in the kitchen.

No. She had to face him. It was the only way to find out what was going on, why he had told Mrs Daley she'd quit her job. But even so, as the door opened, she found herself slinking down in her seat.

Peeking around the arms of the sofa, she watched as a tall, fair-haired woman wrapped in fur embraced Mrs Daley. "Hello, Mother dear."

"Gloria, you're looking too thin."

"Now, mother, don't fuss. Look, Bill has come to see you."

The man who followed Mrs Beaumont in was heavy-set and balding. He spotted Josie at once. "Who's that?"

Gathering her courage, Josie rose. "I'm Josie Morgan." She started to move forward with her right hand extended, but Mr Beaumont drew back. Then he turned to Mrs Daley. "I think we should all have a cup of tea. Perhaps this girl could show me where everything is."

"Would you mind, Josie?" Mrs Daley asked.

Josie realised at once that he wanted to get her alone. As she moved, she felt like she was a condemned prisoner on her final walk. And when she was face-to-face with Mr Beaumont in the kitchen, he looked exactly like an executioner.

He didn't waste any time on small talk. "What are you doing here? I told your mother you were not to see, call, or have any contact with my mother-in-law again."

He kept his voice down, but the anger in it

was apparent. Josie fought the urge to cower.

"I want to know why you told my mother that. And why Mrs Daley thinks I resigned."

His skin darkened. "I told her that to hide the truth from her. Obviously, you had her fooled. She didn't realise that you were trying to use her, to take advantage of her generosity."

"That's not true!" Josie exclaimed. "How can you say that? I'd never do anything to hurt Mrs Daley!"

Could a person's voice be low and thunderous at the same time? Somehow, Mr Beaumont managed it. "I have proof of your intentions, young lady!"

Josie faced him squarely. "Oh yeah?" she challenged him. "What's your proof?" She was amazed to find herself speaking so strongly to a grown-up. But she wasn't going to let this man intimidate her.

"My daughter heard you," Mr Beaumont stated.

Josie stiffened. She should have guessed Heather was behind all this!

He continued. "She heard you asking Mrs Daley for a loan."

As Josie absorbed this, the kitchen door opened. "What's keeping you two?" Mrs Daley asked. Behind her was Mrs Beaumont.

"Nothing, Mother," Mr Beaumont replied smoothly.

"Oh yes, it *is* something," Josie declared. Disregarding the warning look from Mr Beaumont, she said, "Mr Beaumont was just explaining why I was fired."

Mrs Daley was aghast. "Fired! Bill, you fired Josie?"

"He said Heather told him I was trying to get you to give me money."

"But that's ridiculous!" Mrs Daley exclaimed. "Josie never asked me for money."

"Don't defend her, Mother Daley," Mr Beaumont said. "I know you don't like to admit that there's anything bad about a person, but in this case, you have to."

Mrs Daley rapped her cane on the floor so hard Josie could feel the vibrations. "I am telling you that girl never asked me for a dime! In fact, I offered her a loan, several times, and she refused to take it!"

"Bill," Mrs Beaumont murmured, "you know that Mother never lies."

For the first time, Mr Beaumont hesitated. "But, Heather told me—"

"Heather must have misunderstood," Mrs Daley said smoothly. "And I'm quite annoyed with you, Bill, for not telling me all about this in the first place. I could have cleared this up immediately."

Mr Beaumont looked uncertain. "Well, I suppose it's possible that Heather could have misinterpreted what she heard. . . ."

"Precisely," Mrs Daley said. "Now, where's that tea?"

"I'll fix it," Josie said. "Why don't you all go back in the living room and sit down."

She was grateful for a moment alone. She needed it. Although she'd always considered herself a pretty gutsy person, this confrontation had really drained her. And thinking about what Heather had done sent a burning anger through her. But at least the truth was out.

When she brought the tea in, Mrs Daley nudged her son-in-law. Looking slightly abashed, he rose. "Josie, I believe I owe you an apology."

Actually, Josie thought it was Heather who should be offering the apology, but it was highly unlikely she'd ever get one from her. "It's okay."

"Of course, you can have your job back," he added.

Josie considered it. She remembered what Mrs Daley had said about enjoying her daughter's regular visits. And there was something else that had always bothered her. "No, thank you. I never felt right about getting paid for coming here. I'd rather just visit Mrs Daley as a friend."

Mrs Daley seemed pleased, but then she frowned. "Josie, what about your horse?"

Before Josie could respond, Mr Beaumont groaned. "Don't talk about horses." Mrs Beaumont nodded in agreement.

"What do you mean?" Mrs Daley asked.

"Two days ago, out of the blue, Heather asked me to buy her a horse," Mr Beaumont told them.

"Which was very strange," Mrs Beaumont interrupted, "since she's never shown any interest in horses before."

Mr Beaumont went on with his story. "Of course, I wanted to get her a thoroughbred. But for some reason, she insisted on some ten-year-old quarter horse. I don't know what's so special about this animal, but she was adamant."

A cold shiver ran up and down Josie's spine. Strangely, she wasn't at all surprised. "Sunshine."

"Oh, did she tell you about him?" Mrs Beaumont asked.

Mrs Daley's eyebrows shot up. "Josie, was that the horse you wanted to buy?"

Silently, Josie nodded.

"Now, why would Heather suddenly buy the horse you wanted?" Mrs Daley wondered.

If she hadn't been seething with anger, Josie would have smiled. Funny, how family members can know so little about each other.

"Well, anyway," Mr Beaumont continued,

130

"now that she's got her horse, she's shown no interest in him whatsoever. That horse hasn't received any attention or exercise since he arrived."

"Sometimes I think we spoil Heather," Mrs Beaumont said with a sigh.

It was all Josie could do to keep from asking how you could spoil someone who was already rotten.

"A horse has to have attention and exercise," Mrs Daley declared. "You know, that sounds like the perfect job for Josie."

"That's an idea," Mr Beaumont said. "Would you be interested, Josie?"

Josie's first instinct was to refuse. How could she go work for the Beaumont family, when Heather Beaumont had gone out of her way to be the Morgan girls' sworn enemy?

But there was such a thing as cutting off your nose to spite your face.

"Of course, we'll pay you," Mr Beaumont said. "Just what you've been making here."

"More," Mrs Daley commanded. "Taking care of a horse is a lot more work than sitting around talking to an old lady."

"Okay, okay," Mr Beaumont agreed. "How about it, Josie?"

It would mean time with Sunshine, Josie thought. Then there was the money, too. Maybe the Beaumonts would get fed up with Heather's neglect of the horse. Maybe . . . just maybe, someday, they'd want to sell him.

And of course, there was the satisfaction of seeing Heather's reaction when she found Josie in the stable!

When Josie got home, a strange scene greeted her. Becka sat in the rocking chair, grinning from ear to ear. Ben was scowling, scratching his head, and pacing the room. Annie, looking flustered and confused, sat on the arm of the sofa.

"What's going on?" Josie asked. "Why aren't you at the store?"

"We had to close," Annie told her. "We didn't have anything left to sell."

Josie gaped. "What happened? Were we robbed?"

"No," Ben said. "Your sister here happened to tell a reporter from the *Daily News* about her ad. He thought it was a cute story and wrote about it in his column."

"The customers were *pouring* in," Becka finished smugly.

"That's fantastic!" Josie exclaimed. "But Ben, you don't look very happy about it. What's wrong?"

"I can't help feeling we're getting all those customers under false pretenses."

"Nonsense," Annie said. "They're coming

because the article said we had good things to sell."

"But none of this would have happened in the first place if Becka hadn't written that silly ad," Ben argued. "We're benefiting from something she shouldn't have done. The ends don't justify the means."

"Look, you don't have to thank me," Becka said patiently. "And I learned my lesson about false advertising. Why don't we just chalk it up to good fortune?"

Annie laughed. "That sounds like a fine idea to me."

Ben grunted and sank down in a chair. "Doesn't seem right," he muttered. Then he sighed and smiled. "But I guess I'll just have to live with it."

"How do I look?" Cat appeared at the bottom of the stairs, dressed in black velvet. She struck a pose and sauntered across the living room.

"Beautiful, Cat," Annie said. "But what are you wearing it now for?"

"I just wanted to try it on for you." She twirled around. "I still can't believe it's really, truly mine. Of course, I worked hard enough for it."

Josie rolled her eyes.

"Where have you been, by the way?" Annie asked Josie.

"To see Mrs Daley."

Annie was dismayed. "But Josie—"

"Wait," Josie interrupted, then she told them the whole story.

When she finished, Annie shook her head. "Surely Heather couldn't have lied on purpose. I'm sure it was just a misunderstanding, like Mr Beaumont told you."

"Buying the horse, that was probably just a coincidence," Ben added.

Josie, Cat, and Becka exchanged meaningful looks. They knew better.

"Anyway, I've got a new job," she announced. "I'm going to exercise Sunshine."

She was right to try to avoid Cat's eyes. "You can't work for the Beaumonts!" Cat screeched. "Don't you have any pride?"

"I'd trade it in for a horse any day," Josie replied promptly.

Cat opened her mouth to continue her lecture. Then she caught sight of herself in the mirror over the fireplace and forgot all about her sister's disgraceful action.

Ben was staring at his three daughters in bewilderment. "I don't get it. Just this morning, the three of you were miserable. Now you're all happy as clams."

Annie smiled. "Better get used to it, Ben. They're teenagers.

"Can't you just stay like this?" Ben asked hopefully.

"We'll try," Becka said.

"Sure we will," Cat agreed.

Josie just smiled. She knew better. But right this minute, the world seemed bright. The store was back on its feet. Becka had helped get it there. Cat had her dress. As for herself, she didn't have exactly what she'd wanted, but she was closer to it than she'd been before.

Yes, life was good. Not perfect, maybe. But definitely good.

Here's a sneak peek at what's ahead in the exciting sixth book of THREE OF A KIND: *101 Ways to Win Homecoming Queen*

Cat leaned forward. "Guys, we have to think of some way to cheer Marla up."

Britt and Trisha agreed. "But how?" Trisha asked.

"Shh," Britt hissed. "Here she comes now."

Cat turned. "Hey, you know, she doesn't look like she needs cheering up." Marla's expression had changed dramatically since that morning. As she carried her tray to their table, she was greeting people with a bright smile.

"Maybe she's faking it," Britt said.

If so, it was a great performance. Marla was grinning from ear to ear and her eyes were sparkling as she joined them. "Wait till you guys hear this!"

"What happened?" Trisha asked.

Marla sat down. "Guess what I just found stuck on my locker door?"

Cat took a stab at it. "A note?"

Marla nodded.

"From who?" Britt asked eagerly. "Steve Garner?"

Marla wrinkled her nose and shook her head. "Better than Steve Garner."

"Well, that includes about ninety-five per cent of the male student body," Cat said. "C'mon, tell us. Which guy sent you a note?"

Marla grinned mischievously. She was obviously enjoying the suspense. "I didn't say it was a guy."

"Tell us!" Trisha demanded.

Marla laughed. "I'll let you read it. No, I'll read it to you." She extracted a plain white envelope from her purse and pulled out a sheet of paper. She paused dramatically, then began to read.

"To Marla Eastman. From the Student Council."

Cat smiled, but the opening was a letdown. It must be another committee appointment. What was so thrilling about that?

Marla continued, reading slowly, savouring each and every word. "It is our great pleasure to inform you that you have been selected as a nominee for Winter Carnival Princess."

There was a moment of utter silence. Then Britt let out a shriek, and Trisha clapped her hands. Marla happily accepted their congratulations.

"That's fantastic!" Cat exclaimed. It was great seeing Marla look excited and full of life again. But she had a question. "What's a Winter Carnival Princess?"

"It's part of the whole celebration," Britt explained. "There are three nominees, and the school votes on them. The Princess is crowned at the basketball game. It's supposed to be a secret, but it always leaks out before the game."

Cat beamed at Marla. "This should make up for all those bad things that have been happening."

Marla nodded. "Of course, I'm not the Princess yet. I have to be elected."

"You will be," Trisha said with conviction.

"I guess I have a decent chance," Marla said. "But I wonder who the other nominees are."

Cat's eyes roamed around the cafeteria to see if she could spot any other girls looking particularly excited.

"Gee, I hate to leave this celebration, but I have to go to the library," Britt said. "You do, too, Trisha."

"We'll try to find out who the other nominees are," Trisha said as she rose. "See you guys later."

"It doesn't even matter who they are," Cat

assured Marla. "You're going to win. I feel it in my bones. Besides, you're one of the most popular girls at school."

She realised Marla was looking past her, at Heather Beaumont. "Yeah, but there are other popular girls. And some of them are awfully persuasive."

"You think Heather's one of the nominees?"

"I don't know." A look of uncertainty clouded Marla's face.

"Well, there's one way to find out." Cat rose from her seat. Luckily, Heather's table was right by the water fountain. Cat walked over, took a drink, then smiled brightly at the girls gathered around Heather.

"Congratulations," she said.

Heather's cold green eyes met hers. "Are you speaking to me?"

"Well, no, actually, I was congratulating Blair. I heard she's going to be a cheerleader. Is there some reason I should be congratulating you, too?"

Two of the girls started giggling. Heather smiled smugly. "Oh, you'll find out sooner or later." And then Cat spotted it – a plain white envelope, identical to Marla's, lying by Heather's tray.

Cat went back to her own table and reported what she had seen to Marla. She watched all the happiness evaporate from Marla's face.

"Oh, well," Marla said with a sigh. "I guess it was nice being nominated."

"Cut that out," Cat said firmly. "Stop being so negative! Just because Heather was nominated doesn't mean she's going to win."

"She beat me when we ran against each other for pep club vice-president last year," Marla reminded her. "And she kept me from becoming a cheerleader."

"So what? The whole school is voting, remember? You've got more friends than Heather."

"Yeah, but for some reason Heather always gets her way."

"Not this time," Cat said with determination. "I always get my way, too, you know." She thought for a minute. "I'll get my sisters to help. Josie can pull in the basketball vote. Becka can work on the brains. And *I'll* get everyone else!"

A tiny smile began to form on Marla's face. "You think you've got that much influence?"

Cat didn't have to fake any modesty around Marla. "There isn't anything I've wanted bad enough that I couldn't get if I worked at it. And I've decided I want you to be Winter Carnival Princess."

She was pleased to see the effect her words had on Marla. She wore a real smile now, and a little of that old self-assurance had returned to her eyes. "Gee, Cat, I don't know what I'd do without you. You're a real friend. You're really going to help me get this?"

"I promise." Cat got up. "I have to run by my locker before class. I'll call you tonight and we'll start planning our strategy."

Annie's right, Cat thought as she left the cafeteria. It *did* give her a nice feeling inside, knowing she could help Marla get something she wanted so much. It was almost as nice as getting something for herself. Besides, Marla's grumpy mood was beginning to get on her nerves.

"Cat, wait up!" Becka appeared by her side. "This is so depressing. I've asked a dozen kids if they'd want a little sister. Nobody's showing the least bit of interest."

"That was a dumb promise you made to Michelle. And besides," Cat continued, "you can't expect people to want a kid they've never even seen."

Becka nodded. "Maybe I can ask Ben and Annie if she can visit on Saturday. Then we could take her to the basketball game and show her around."

"There you go, saying 'we' again," Cat said. "This is *your* problem, not mine."

"Come on, Cat, you've got to help me," Becka wheedled. "I'll bet you're going to need *my* help one of these days."

Cat recalled the conversation she'd just had

141

with Marla. "You know, for once in your life, you're right. There's something I do need your help with." She told Becka about Marla's nomination for Winter Carnival Princess. "I promised her we'd help getting her elected."

"Fine," Becka said promptly. "You help me find a family for Michelle, and I'll help get votes for Marla."

"All right," Cat said. "It's a deal."

"Hey, there's something on your locker," Becka said.

Cat stood very still. Becka was right. Taped to her locker door was a familiar-looking, plain white envelope. She stared at it in disbelief.

"Aren't you going to see what it is?" Becka asked.

Cat could feel her heartbeat speeding up as she ripped the envelope off her locker. She opened it and pulled out a sheet of paper.

Becka read aloud over her shoulder. "To Catherine Morgan. From the Student Council. It is our great pleasure to inform you that you have been selected as a nominee for Winter Carnival Princess."

Reading the words and hearing them at the same time still didn't make them real. Cat read the lines over and over, checking to make sure that it was really her name on top. A tingle started in her toes and shot all the way up through her entire body. She could almost

142

feel the Winter Carnival Princess crown on her head. She was dizzy, she was floating, she was riding on a cloud.

She turned to Becka in ecstasy. But Becka wasn't smiling. Her words brought Cat back down to earth with a thud.

"*Now* who's making dumb promises. Still want me to help get votes for Marla?"